I0700006

CURSED MAGIC

SHADOW COVEN
BOOK ONE

Cursed Magic
Shadow Coven Book 1
Heather Young-Nichols

All rights reserved.
Copyright © 2022 Heather Young-Nichols
Print ISBN: 979-8-9862760-3-8

No part of this book may be reproduced, distributed transmitted in any form or by any means, or stored in a database retrieval system without the prior writer permission from the author. You must not circulate this book in any format. Thank you for respecting the rights of the author. This is a work of fiction. Names, characters, businesses, organizations, places, events, and incidents are either the products of the author's imagination or used in a fictitious manner. Any resemblance to actual persons, living or dead, or actual events is purely coincidental.

heatheryoungnichols.com

ALSO BY HEATHER YOUNG-NICHOLS

Rules of the Game

Kissing the Player

Wanting the Player

Moonstruck

Moonstruck

Moontouched

The Empowered Series

The Gremlin Prince

The Goblin War

The Gorgon Sacrifice

Shadow Coven

Haunted Magic

Cursed Magic

Stolen Magic

Fated Magic

Forever 18

Forever Grayson

Forever London

Forever Lennox

Heavy Hitter

Pushing Daisies

Daisy

Van

Bonham

Daltrey

Mack

Courting Chaos

Cross

Ransom

Booker

Dixon

Finding Love

Making Her Mine

Making Him Hers

Harbor Point

Love by the Slice

Love by the Mile

Love by the Rules

Gambling on Love

Highest Bidder

Highest Stakes

Highest Reward

Holiday Bites

All I Want

All of Me

The Fallout Series

Last Good Thing

Last First Kiss

Last Chance Love

With J.A. Hardt

Bound by Magic

With Amelia J. Matthews

Dirt on the Diamond

After Office Hours: Seducing the Professor

1

MILLER

The tree branch beside me fell with a thunderous crack.

Shit. That was close.

"Do you see them?" Luken, one of my best friends and fellow witch, called out.

"I don't."

Oliver cursed, then said, "I don't, either."

The three of us couldn't see each other, but thanks to a spell Oliver had found, we had a supernatural communication system running for this. Cell phones required service. Even those ear things that security people used needed electricity.

Service and electricity were two things we couldn't guarantee when going up against other witches. A simple spell could wipe them all out.

"Hold on," Luken whispered, bringing me to a stop. I didn't move, tried not to breathe too loudly, and assumed Oliver would be doing the same. "Fuck."

A slew of words that, put together, created a spell followed.

I took off in a run in the direction I'd last seen Luken. The woods were so dense that I couldn't even see the light from his magic until I was closer. Oliver popped out of the other side.

The two of us began our own spells, the magic zipping from our fingertips.

We didn't have wands, we had words. Still, certain spells created a flow that emanated from us. A bright white or blue, usually.

I grounded myself to the elements so each spell I casted would have more power. The wind picked up, swirling much like a tornado. When Luken and Oliver realized what I was doing, they joined in. Their magic mingled with mine as the three of us carefully inched closer to create the triangle. Between all of our magic, the two dark witches in the clearing didn't stand a chance.

The swirling wind encapsulated the spells they were throwing at us. It also thinned the air. I'd started this spell just to contain them but soon both dropped to the dirt and didn't move.

"Fuck." Luken's voice was as breathless as mine felt. "I hate this shit."

"By 'this shit,' do you mean the shadow coven?" Oliver asked with humor in his voice.

"Yes."

"Yeah," I agreed. "I don't think any of us exactly love the fact that we have to chase these assholes down when they get too close."

"You know they're dead, right?" he asked.

Nodding, I quickly wet my lips. "Yeah. I don't love it, but what else were we supposed to do? Though, to be honest, that wasn't my plan when I called on Air."

Oliver turned to me and crossed his arms over his chest. "What did you plan on happening, then?"

I shrugged and threw my hands up in the air. "Make sure you two didn't die."

Luken snorted as he began walking toward the two witches on the ground. "Because somehow, you wouldn't be affected, right?"

I gave him a wide grin. "I *am* the strongest witch here."

"Fuck that." Oliver scoffed.

"Yeah, I don't think so, buddy," added Luken.

"It's OK that both of you are wrong."

The two of them chuckled while I followed them.

We stood over the bodies of the witches, both of whom were young, male, and very, very dead.

"Guess we have to call Michael," I told them.

"Not it!" They both called out at the same time.

Fuck them.

None of us wanted to call the head of the council, but it had to be done. We had protocols to take care of this sort of thing and there were a couple of higher-level spells that might allow the council to get some information on the dead.

I could've performed the spell. Hell, any of the three of us could have, but not a single one wanted to flirt with necromancy. That was a nasty business that we'd happily leave to the elders.

"You guys are assholes." I pulled out my phone and placed the call so that these bodies wouldn't be lying here for some random hiker to find.

It was one of the ways we kept Echo Valley as a whole from discovering that a coven of witches lived among them.

"You work tomorrow?" Luken asked as the three of us headed back toward town.

The cleanup crew was on their way and there was no reason for us to stick around.

"Yup."

"Guess I'll see you at the garage in the morning," Oliver called out as he took off toward his car.

It was already morning if you wanted to get technical, but I could still get a few hours of sleep.

I was going to need it, considering the old car waiting at the garage in the morning.

Three hours wasn't enough but it'd have to do.

The coffee I downed like it was air helped a little and I knew the caffeine would kick in quickly. Then it was off to work.

Two hours later, I'd been working on the longest screw to ever go into a car in the history of cars. It was so long that it was like the thing was trying to screw me and as I kept turning the head, it probably wasn't going to be long before I felt it brushing against my skin.

The damn thing was so hard to get out that I figured the threads at the end had to be stripped. Though how that would happen, the gods only knew.

The chatter around the garage was like background music to me at this point. I'd grown up around this place since it was my dad's garage, but it was also sort of a fortress of solitude where the men didn't watch their words unless a customer came in.

Sure, the guys talked about whom they'd gone out with last night. We knew when sex happened and all of that, but my dad wouldn't tolerate any of us being disrespectful to women. It was his thing. If he knew that anyone had done or said anything about a woman that was "off-color," as he put it, there would've been hell to pay.

His sister had disappeared when he'd been younger and they'd never found her. I figured it had to have something to do with that, but he wouldn't talk about it. Neither would his parents. She was gone and that was all the information that I was going to get.

"Miller," Luken McCormack called out.

When I pushed out from under the hood, he waved me over. Neither of us looked or acted like we'd been out until three this morning dispatching a couple of dark witches.

I had to grab a rag off the bumper of the car for my very greasy hands before heading over to him.

Luken and Oliver Coleman were my closest friends, though I'd known Oliver longer. We'd started kindergarten together, while Luken had come to Echo Valley in high school. Still, the three of us had formed our little trio while Oliver and I had helped Luken learn his magic.

His mother had hidden the fact that he was a witch, so when he'd gotten to town, he'd been out of control. Bad shit had happened anywhere he was. He'd had no idea how to control it. The council had put him under our care and tasked us with teaching him the basics.

We were naturals at teaching, I supposed, because, in no time, he was a seasoned witch.

"What's up?" I asked him.

Luken and I were the same height, same size. The only difference was that his eyes and hair were dark. Sometimes his eyes were so dark, I couldn't make out the pupil. While my hair was a medium blond and I had these weird, icy-blue eyes that neither of my parents had. Ladies swooned for them, but they were so clear, they could be off-putting, even to me, when I glanced in the mirror.

A genetic anomaly that happened to witches sometimes, my mother had told me. And I wasn't the only one. Our coven leader, Michael, had the same blip in his DNA.

"The council wants to see you."

"Fuck," I muttered.

That usually meant you were either in trouble or

they had a job for you to do. Neither of which was a particularly exciting option at the moment. I just wanted to finish the car and be done for the day.

It was late enough in the afternoon that if I'd finished up with this car, Tommy, our boss, wouldn't have me start another just to leave it for tomorrow. I'd probably clock out, be gone, and have a shower and a beer before seeing what Oliver and Luken wanted to do tonight.

"What do they want?" I asked as I walked back to the sink to clean up. Since our boss was a witch too, he knew that when the council called, you went. Didn't matter what else you had going on.

Our coven was a light coven. Light magic was good magic. Dark magic was bad. That had been drilled into our brains since the beginning. Each of us had chosen the light and it had been clear it was a choice. It was a whole thing.

There was so much going on that we didn't know about, it was hard to guess why the council might call you in.

Right now, I'd heard rumblings about untrained, unaffiliated descendants of the Salem witches and the Michigan witches, but that was all I'd heard. Rumblings. I seriously hoped the council wasn't about to send me off to train another newbie. Talk about a headache. I'd rather snuff out shadow coven witches than start over with a new one.

Or I was perfectly happy to stay home and fix cars.

"They didn't say," Luken explained. "Danna called and said they wanted to see you."

"I haven't done anything wrong or sort of wrong in a while, so it's got to be a job." I groaned internally.

"Yeah." He sighed. "It's probably just a job. Not a big deal." Though he didn't sound convinced, which meant I wouldn't be, either. Not until I talked to them

"You want to walk or drive?" I asked.

We weren't far from the council building and if Luken was called to bring me in, then he'd have to go there with me. Have to at least watch me go through the door. It was the buddy system so that no witch would consider ignoring the summons. They always sent a friend to escort you. Because if you took off, the friend would get in trouble too.

It was easier to just follow the rules. Following the rules lengthened whatever leash the coven had on you. They didn't control us but there was an understanding by being part of the coven and that included you being there when they needed you.

"May as well walk. It's a nice day."

I nodded, let my dad know that I'd been summoned, and headed out.

We took a right on the sidewalk but didn't rush. Hey, the summons meant I had to go there and I couldn't waste time. It didn't mean we had to full-out run.

"What do you think they want me to do?" I asked him as we made our way. "Gather some supplies for a ritual? That'd be the easiest thing they could ask."

Luken snorted. "Probably not. Why wouldn't they just have one of their underlings do that?" "Underlings" referred to those who wanted to be on the council one day who worked for them now basically as interns.

Fuck, they worked those witches to the bone.

"Some of them just started. Maybe the council doesn't trust them yet."

He raised an eyebrow at me then shook his head. "You're kidding me, right? The underlings might've just started, but they grew up here, remember? If the council didn't trust them, they wouldn't be there."

We passed Luken's apartment building and then took a left.

The sun was high and to the outside eye, Echo Valley looked like any other small town in America.

It just happened that this small town was the settlement of the largest light witch coven in the United States. Maybe the world. I didn't know. My parents didn't talk about other covens and neither did the council. At least not to me.

"You see Oliver this morning?" I asked when we turned onto the street of the council building.

"Nope. You know he needs his beauty sleep."

I snorted.

"Hey," he said before I could form a response. "Didn't you go out with what's-her-name the other night?"

I groaned. "Don't remind me."

How easily I'd forgotten the most boring date of my life with Morgan. She was nice and all that, but there'd been zero attraction once we'd gotten to know each other a little. And that went both ways.

"That's what I get for dating a non-witch," I added. He knew that it'd been shit.

"Yeah, but can you imagine if we only went out with witches from our coven?"

I snorted. "Not really. One of us would end up dating Mildred Cunningham." She was the oldest member of our coven, and she didn't do much magic anymore.

It didn't help that I wasn't about to have a relationship with anyone and that might've been the problem with my last date. It was like the universe was telling me to never give my heart to anyone.

No one understood my weird take on love, as they called it but it was a feeling I couldn't shake. I grew up in a stable house with parents who were devoted to each other. They'd never had any more kids after me, though I didn't know why and thought there was probably a story there.

But the idea of being in love didn't appeal to me. It was like a lump in my chest that I couldn't explain but I was a firm believer in trusting your gut and mine told me that a relationship wasn't in my future.

"What's taking you guys so long?" Danna was standing outside of the council building with her dark hair pulled back into a bun and her arms over her chest, her pale skin extra bright in the sunlight. The impatient tap of her foot against the sidewalk told me she'd been there since she'd made the call, as if I'd magically appear in an instant. It was cute though. Here she was a good five inches shorter than me, weighing maybe a hundred pounds soaking wet, yet she looked like an impatient elementary school teacher ready to give me a talking down.

We'd gone to high school with Danna Payne and hung out in the same group. Luken also may or may not have hooked up with her senior year. OK, he had, but I wasn't supposed to know that. Now Danna worked with the council and was the newest and youngest member of the council.

She'd wanted on the council more than anything else when we'd been kids. It'd been her one goal, even though it sounded like a damned nightmare to me. To her, it was a chance to make a difference for our community. If we weren't witches, she'd probably run for president one day.

"'So long'?" I asked. "We headed right here after he got the call."

She shook her head as Luken shifted his weight. Whatever had happened between the two of them had left things slightly uncomfortable. "Rough day?" he asked.

"Not exactly." She sighed then pinched the bridge of her nose for a few seconds. "More long than rough."

"That's what she said," I muttered under my breath, making her laugh loudly.

Danna was incredibly pretty with big, light-brown eyes with specks of gold. I didn't know why I knew that detail about her, but here we were. The kindness she exuded, to everyone except Luken, was the best part of her. If she and Luken had gotten together more permanently, I wouldn't have been mad about it.

"What's going on in there?" I asked once she'd settled down.

"Waiting for you. Once we're done with you, we're done and I'd love nothing more than to not spend the rest of my day hanging out with these old guys in dark rooms. I'm kind of over it for now."

"Hey." I snapped my fingers as she and I started walking toward the door.

Luken could come in—well, not into the room with me, but into the building—he'd just chosen not to once we'd crossed the threshold. If he had, he'd risk getting sent on another job that could keep him away for months. That had been the agreement when we'd joined the coven as adults. Everyone had to do their share to keep the thing working.

"I never heard if you convinced them to bind the mind-reading garbage." It was something she'd mentioned when she'd first gotten the invitation to work with the council, but she hadn't mentioned it since.

Certain members could read minds. Michael specifically and it was creepy as hell. Danna had told me one night at a party that she was going to suggest they bind it since so many of us found it unsettling.

Since she was a new member, it probably wouldn't have been taken well.

"Right." She stopped and turned so that the two of us were in a little huddle and no one else would hear us. "No one is supposed to know, so if you tell Luken, he has to be aware of the fact that he can't tell anyone else. But yes. I convinced them to bind it. It was really only Michael anyway, so he fought it, but I told them I didn't think it was fair for one person to know our every thought when we didn't know his, especially when it came to voting for what's best for the coven."

"He went for that?" Luken asked.

"I said that as a condition of joining the council it was either that or he was required to teach us all how to do it. And since they had to have another permanent voting member, and no one was volunteering..." She wet her bottom lip. "He chose the binding with the condition that we not make the entire coven aware because he thinks people will be more apt to deceive us if they think he can't hear their inner thoughts."

"There's always a truth spell."

"That's what I said. So, it's done." Her brown eyes settled on me. "You're safe with your thoughts, but I promise you, this isn't a big deal. Just something that needs to be done."

It took my eyes several moments to adjust to the contrast of the darkness from the bright sun outside. Why they kept it so dim, I had no idea and Danna must not have, either, because she groaned and rubbed her own eyes.

"I swear to you," she whispered. "When the old crew dies out and I'm in charge, we are at least going to have forty-watt lightbulbs in this place."

I snorted. "You want to be in charge one day?"

"Yes. Now that I'm in this, I want the coven to be taken care of and I want to see some change." She glanced at me then focused back down the hall. "You, Oliver... Luken... You can all help me and we can bring this coven into the twenty-first century."

"Or at least the twentieth." Because our coven still had so many old ways. While some of them were good, we were modern-day witches. We didn't need dark, dank meeting places. "Hey." I stopped her from opening the meeting room door made of thick wood so that no one could eavesdrop right outside.

"What?" she whispered back.

"Where's your robe?" I asked her.

For as long as I could remember, the council wore these long, black robes in the meeting room.

But Danna was entering in her flowered skirt, sandals, and tank top.

"It's not required and think of it as me bringing us into the present."

Then she pushed through. It was weird to think that this young woman, only twenty-one years old, was powerful enough to push back against the council that had been running our coven for so many years. Michael, I was told, had joined around twenty years ago. Since we weren't immortal, we all knew that the council as it currently was would come to an end probably all at once, given that the other four were all around the same age.

I stepped in after her and while she scurried over to the long table, I took a seat in the lone chair waiting for me. The room had no lights on, but about a million candles illuminated the area. Again, trying to make everything even creepier than it needed to be.

Maybe they didn't realize the rest of us wouldn't hate coming here if it didn't look like a medieval torture chamber.

"Thank you for coming, Miller." Michael, the oldest-looking and head of the council greeted me.

As if I had a choice was how I wanted to answer, but instead, I said, "Of course."

"As you know, we have a lot that needs to be done at the moment. The shadow coven is growing and becoming a bigger problem."

"How do I fit in?" I asked, daring to keep Michael on track.

His icy eyes settled on me. His hair looked like someone had brushed white paint through it and there was nothing about him warm or welcoming. Thank the gods he couldn't hear my thoughts anymore. That was a witch skill that should have been bred out a long time ago.

"We need you to shadow..." Danna looked down at the paper before her. "Hazel Reilly."

Fuck. "Uh... not a good idea." And Danna would've known that, given that we'd been in the same class since kindergarten.

Danna held back a smile. She was enjoying my discomfort, but she knew that Hazel hated my ass and I wasn't too fond of her, either.

"Are you saying you won't do this?" Michael's voice boomed in the quiet room. Danna raised an eyebrow.

It was nice having a friendly face amongst the not-so-friendly ones.

"I'm not saying that, but she hates me. Like, *really* hates me."

"There have been other witches who have hated each other, yet they find a way to work together," Danna countered. "Nobody said you have to be best friends."

Yeah, there was no chance of that happening. I might not have stabbed her with a pencil like Oliver had done to one of our classmates—on accident, of course—but there was no love lost between Hazel and me not seeing each other for ages.

I only wished that when they said "shadow," it just meant to watch her, but I knew better. I'd have to interact with the one person on this planet who hated my ass the most.

2

———

HAZEL

Damn it.

It happened again.

I was alone in my bedroom, trying to get ready for work and I couldn't find my damn phone. It had to be there somewhere. But I was beginning to think my house was haunted.

Dumb, right? Ghosts weren't real.

Yet at some point between when I'd gone into my closet to see if I'd somehow left it there, the blanket on my bed had ended up on the floor. I hadn't done it. So what was the explanation?

Stuff like that had been happening for a while and the only explanation that I could come up with was ghosts or gremlins.

Neither of which existed.

"Where the hell are you?" I whispered, as if my phone could hear, understand, and respond.

Please let me find you. I can't be late."

I prayed to myself to find the thing. Yeah, it was a dumb thing to wish the universe would help me out with, but I needed my phone and I couldn't be late.

That was when I felt something in my back pocket and sure enough, it was my phone. Which absolutely had not been there moments before.

"Thanks, gremlin or ghost, for the assist." There was no way I wouldn't have felt my phone in my pocket as I'd been looking, but I wasn't going to waste time thinking about it.

So far, the unseen resident of my room hadn't caused any harm, so I was going to continue to ignore it and go to work.

Once I got in, my day went well for the most part. So well that I should've known something was going to screw it up and I would've rather it have been a sharp stick in the eye.

Instead, my father came into the bookstore where I worked and ruined everything good about the day. It was like my parents had the natural ability to suck the good out of everything around them.

Why had he come in? Because, apparently, as

their child, my lot in life was to have it ruined by either him or my mother.

Here I was minding my own business at work, Pick-a-Book Bookstore, when he decided there was a need to talk to me right now. Later wasn't good enough. As if I didn't get enough of their judgment, pressure, and disappointment at home.

"Hazel, we have to talk to you," my father said as he came through the door without checking to see if there were any other customers in the place. He didn't care if I was, you know, working.

My last customer had left several minutes before, but he didn't know that.

"I'm working," I told him, knowing that wouldn't cut it. Whatever he had going on was clearly much more important than my measly job.

I couldn't wait to get away from them permanently.

Dad was tall with red hair like mine, though mine was brighter because it wasn't brushed with gray like his. His eyes were brown and mine were jade like Mom's, but she had blonde hair. So I supposed I was a mix between the two. I was also on the short side, like Mom. I'd read once that the red hair-green eye combo was among the rarest and thought that at least my parents had given me something good.

I thought Dad liked being so much bigger than most people, but especially me because he tried to use his size to intimidate me. It never worked. Don't get me wrong. That man's temper could scare the crap out of the toughest man, but I didn't let it intimidate me.

"There's no one here." Though he hadn't looked around at all.

I took a deep breath and planted my feet. "I have other things to do. What do you want?"

"Your mother told you about the function we'd like you to attend."

"She did. I politely declined."

I'd continue to decline as long as they asked because I wasn't sure why this event was so much more important than the last, but either way, I wasn't going. I'd never gone to one of their things... I honestly didn't even know what it was about, so why would I go now?

I'd started to think it was a fundraiser because those tended to be important to them and unlike a lot of people in Echo Valley, my parents had money. Money that I didn't personally like to flaunt in people's faces, not that keeping it quiet had helped me in high school.

But that was another story.

They didn't seem to mind if people knew they had money. Dad had invented this software forever ago and the payments kept rolling in. He still worked, from home, but preferred Mom to remain unemployed so that she could bend to his schedule.

When I'd said I was going away to college, all hell had broken loose and the only way Dad would pay for it was if I attended Huron State, which I could commute to. His problem seemed to be more with me moving out than the college I was attending. And I didn't make enough yet to support myself.

I was working on it. I planned to get a job in the city, where I'd make more money and go to school part-time. I'd need loans to do it, but right now, loans wouldn't be enough. I needed to have the income to support me when I wasn't in school. Without income, I'd starve.

Baby steps.

"Why does it matter if I go?" I asked him. It was the question that never really got answered.

"Because we asked."

"Not good enough, Pops. I don't want to attend.

Therefore, if you want me to, I need a reason. That's how it works." I twirled my finger in the air to demonstrate the circle of life or, rather, the circle of logic.

My father clenched his jaw together and took such a deep breath that his nostrils flared. "It's a function and we'd like you there to begin meeting our friends. There will be people your age in attendance. You might make some friends."

"I have friends."

"Appropriate friends," he countered.

Dad didn't like my friends because they didn't have money like we did, but I didn't care about any of that. Or at least I assumed he was a snob about money since he rarely gave me the full story about anything. My friends were great so it had to be the money.

I'd tried explaining it to certain people in high school, but it hadn't been good enough. Thankfully, my biggest nemesis had graduated two years before me and I hadn't had to see him for half my high school career. Miller Campbell had been a nightmare that I'd been glad to be rid of and to this day, I actively avoided him in town.

"Well, again, thanks for the invitation, but I think I'll pass."

"Hazel." He was suddenly so close to me that our

noses almost touched. His hands were pressing against the counter near the register and if he'd had superstrength, I was pretty sure that counter would have been in splinters. "I have asked you nicely. Please do not make me force you."

Whatever Dad thought he was doing, it wasn't going to work. Unfortunately for him, I'd gotten my temper and stubbornness from him.

"And I said *no*." I spat the words out through a tight jaw without moving away from him because I wouldn't give him the satisfaction of backing down.

There was a loud noise down one of the aisles, like several books had fallen off the shelf, and I thought it would be appropriate if the books had responded to my anger. As if they'd known what I was feeling and acted accordingly.

If only. Then one of them would fly through the air and smack my father in the head. That was what I *really* wanted to happen.

With no one else in the store, he could've reached out and slapped me across the face and no one would've known. He wouldn't do it, though, because it'd leave a mark and people would ask questions.

I bruised like a peach.

He'd never hit me once in his life. This was more

about control, but control over a specific area of my life. Otherwise, I had no restrictions. He didn't like my friends, but he never tried to stop me from having them. He didn't like how I spent my time but never micromanaged it. He hated that I worked in this bookstore because he viewed it as beneath us, but he never tried to force me to quit.

He was just desperate for me to become part of this group he and my mom spent a lot of time with. Which set off all the warning bells inside me and told me to steer clear. The more they wanted something, the farther I ran from it. Call it gut instinct. Call it knowing them too well.

"We'll talk about this when you get home."

I raised an eyebrow and fought the urge to roll my eyes before wryly telling him, "Look forward to it."

My dad left the store as if nothing had passed between us and I was left with all the anger boiling inside of me. Anger that I couldn't do much about right now.

I wondered if I could get him banned from the store. I probably could have, but he only came in when I was alone, so who would've enforced it?

At home, I would've gone for a run or angry-texted my friends about what an asshole my dad was. If none of them were busy, then maybe we would've gotten together to vent in person over coffee.

Instead, I stomped my way into the back room, where I kept my personal belongings, and yanked my laptop out of my bag then headed back out front to watch the store. This wasn't even something he'd know I was doing, but I knew. That was enough.

I brought up the website I'd been using to apply for jobs and searched for bookstores in the city. I could work there—full-time if possible—then go to school on the side. Sure, it'd take me longer to get that degree, but I didn't care. Whatever got me away from them the quickest.

Hell, for all I knew, our relationship would be a lot better if there was some distance between us.

It could happen. Then they'd know they had no control over my life, which they hadn't acknowledged since I'd taken that control away at the age of twelve. That was when I started putting my foot down and rejecting some of the things they wanted me to do.

They'd been trying to get me to join their club since I'd been a teenager, but I'd refused again and again. For whatever reason, probably one I should have been suspicious of, they'd never tried to force me into it. I had the sneaking suspicion that they wanted me to choose their life and one way of pushing that choice was by promising that there would be young men at the gatherings.

Like they were trying to marry me off to the man who offered the most goats.

It was crazy and something inside me told me to stay as far away as I could.

So I did.

I hit *enter* on an application and then filled out a second. The city wasn't far. Just, like, an hour away, so I could drive in for any interviews if necessary. After all, I had a brand-new car that Mom and Dad had given me for graduation. A little gray Chevy that would make the trip utterly delightful.

The bell on the door rang, which caused me to slam my laptop closed, as if someone had just caught me doing something I shouldn't have been. I'd started here three years ago and it was going to hurt telling my boss that I was leaving.

"Let me know if there's anything I can help you with," I told the thirty-ish-year-old woman with short, blonde hair when she'd come in. Relief washed over me that it wasn't my boss.

"Actually, I am looking for a particular book," she said as she pulled a piece of paper out of her back pocket. "My friend told me that I absolutely have to read this."

She handed over the paper. Yup. This was the most popular new release. It was supposed to be a super-dirty romance in the BDSM world that was scandalizing the mommy porn industry. There was a new one every year. But I'd read it and eh. Didn't seem like that big of a deal to me.

"This one is right up front." I waved for her to follow when I came out from behind the counter. "I'll show you."

We went around the stack, which was when I noticed a pile of books on the floor between this one and another. *Shoot.* I'd forgotten about that. I'd have to come back once I finished helping her.

"It's right here." I grabbed the book and held it out to her. "We have it in hardcover and paperback." She smiled, so I did too.

"Yeah. I think I'll do hardcover because we're going to read it and discuss it. I just have to catch up." She looked up at me. "If that makes sense."

"Makes total sense to me. My friends and I do that kind of thing all the time." Which wasn't even a lie. My group of friends liked to read just as much as I did. Sometimes we read the same things and sometimes we didn't. Then we'd talk about it. Actually, we talked about books most of the time we saw each other.

"Is there anything else I can find for you today?"

People came into Echo Valley from the surrounding areas because we were one of the best indie bookstores within fifty miles. We carried books that were indie-published right along with the ones that were traditionally published because who cared what company had published the book if people wanted to read it?

So they could make the drive and walk out of our store with a book in hand that the chains wouldn't even carry. It worked for us and kept the doors open.

"I don't think so, but I'll be back if there is."

I didn't recognize her, which meant she didn't live here. We were a small town and if you didn't know someone personally, you usually recognized them, but with her, I just didn't. We weren't so small that everyone knew everyone, though. We had a grocery store and a tiny movie theater that played mostly old movies, but it worked for us.

"No problem. I'll slip a card in your bag that lists our hours and you can always call to see if we carry a book before coming in if you prefer, though we'd always love to see you."

She laughed politely. "Thank you."

After she looked around some more, she was at the registers where I scanned the books she'd picked out and gave her the total. She paid, and then once they were in the bag, she was on her way.

Now it was time to wait for the next customer to arrive.

Oh, shoot. No. I needed to go clean up that pile of books that was lying on the floor between stacks. I'd forgotten once and had almost forgotten again.

I dropped to my knees to stack the books up neatly so that I could more easily organize them for the shelf. It looked like the entire top shelf of this stack just decided to plummet to its death on the floor. OK. I was being dramatic. But they all had fallen for some reason.

After testing out the shelf to make sure it was in good working order, I placed the books back, in order, three at a time. I still didn't know why they'd fallen, but I'd watch to see if it happened again.

Right as I finished up, the bell above the door rang again.

"Welcome to Pick-a-Book. Can I h—"

No. This couldn't have been happening. I'd thought my day couldn't get any worse after my dad had shown up, but once again, the universe had decided to show its weird sense of humor. He could not be in my store while I was working. As a matter of fact, I didn't think he'd ever been in here before.

So why now?

Miller Campbell was taller than he had been the last time I'd seen him. Of course, that had been three years ago. Again, you'd think in a town this size, I would've seen him around and now that I was thinking about it, I knew I was lying to myself to say I hadn't run into him at all.

I'd seen him in town several times, though not as many as you'd think. I'd just made sure that he didn't see me. The memories I carried that included him needed to remain buried. Deep. More than six feet down in a coffin made of lead.

But this was the first time in a long time I was seeing him up close. He was taller, broader-shouldered, and his blond hair wasn't as long. It was still messy and reminded me of when I'd been fifteen.

I shook my head. We were not going to revisit that.

He was wearing jeans and a gray T-shirt. The jeans were well worn and none of it should've reminded me just how attracted I'd been to him back then.

That was a waste of time.

The only thing I should've been thinking about

right now was why in the hell Miller Campbell was standing in front of me in my store.

That was the question that needed to be answered and that answer had better be that he was in desperate need of a specific book.

3

MILLER

THE COUNCIL HAD JUST GIVEN ME MARCHING ORDERS that, for the first time in my coven life, I wanted to ignore, no matter the consequence.

Instead of doing that, I went to see my dad. He'd known about my crush on Hazel in high school and would be able to advise me on what to do next. Even if she'd thought she was better than the rest of us because her father had money, I'd still thought about her on those lonely teen nights.

Now that I was years away from that world, I'd become less certain about that.

"Dad," I called out when I got into the house. He would've been home by then because though it hadn't seemed like I'd been with the council long, they'd kept me for a while to make sure I understood the assignment.

"Kitchen," he called out.

I found him closing the refrigerator with a bunch of vegetables in his arms. I guessed he was making dinner tonight.

"What'd they want you to do?" he asked as soon as he saw me. Someone must've told him where I had headed earlier.

"I'm supposed to shadow Hazel and teach her the craft. At first, I was hoping they just wanted me to get information on her, but no." I took a deep breath. "Did you know she was a witch?"

He nodded as he popped a baby carrot in his mouth.

I looked nothing like my dad. He was all dark, like Luken, and honestly, it didn't make sense. Personality-wise was another story.

He was a big guy, roughly my size, but it was so striking how different we looked. He was all dark and I was blonde with these freaky blue eyes. I wasn't even Mom's color blonde, either, because hers was strongly strawberry. Not red like Hazel's.

"I knew. But her parents chose to bind her powers, so there was no point in telling you."

I scoffed. "I still think it would've been good information to have."

Dad put down the knife he'd just picked up. "It wouldn't have mattered. You couldn't have told her. She would've thought you were out of your mind. She doesn't even know witches exist."

I groaned and dropped my head back. "You've got to be kidding me."

"Nope." His lips popped on the P. "But it doesn't matter, Miller. You're going to go in and do your job. Forget about all of that high school shit. I've been into the bookstore. Hazel is a nice girl who needs your help and protection right now."

"Protection?"

Dad cringed. "I mean to choose the light. We need her on our side."

I let go of the fact that his response didn't make sense. Making sure she chose the light meant she needed guidance. Not protection, but I felt like there was more Dad wasn't saying.

He was big on protection. Protecting those weaker than us or who just need help.

"How am I supposed to make sure she discovers her powers the right way if she doesn't even know that witches exist?"

"You've taught others. Luken, for example. You got this, son."

Dad knew exactly what the problem was—he just wasn't saying it. We might not have looked alike, but we sure as hell thought alike. "You know what the problem is. She fucking hates me."

He nodded. "She might, but that's your problem to fix. You have to do this for the coven. And for her. If the council is sending you, unless you want to fight back against them, I don't know how you can get around it. But it means that they think you're the right person for the job."

"I'm not *trying* to fight them. I'll do it, but I don't think it's going to go well. Once she gets her powers, she's going to turn me into a damn frog."

Dad chuckled as he returned to chopping the vegetables. "I take it you still have feelings for her."

"What?" I snapped. "No. It's not about that."

"It was about that before."

I took a deep breath to calm my nerves. It was like Dad was plucking at every single one on purpose. "Yeah. It was and I regret telling you anything ever. Don't you have other kids to go bother?"

He laughed so loudly that while we were in the

kitchen, I knew Mom could hear him all the way on the other side of the house. "No."

"This is why you should've had more kids." My parents were still married, which in my friend group was a little odd. Luken's mom was dead. His dad... we have no idea. Oliver's dad had died when we'd been little. Talk about dark days. That left me. Happily married parents.

"Seriously, son, if you have to make some apologies, do it. She probably deserves it."

Damn, he knew me too well. "What do you mean?"

"I mean..." He took two big steps toward me. "I don't know everything that happened between the two of you, but I know how you were back then and the girl probably deserves a few apologies."

Having him point out the truth was why I was happy to have my own apartment. OK. It was above my parents' garage, but whatever. It was mine. I paid rent. Though I wasn't dismissive because my dad was wrong or anything.

I was irritated that he was right. I seemed to remember words like "princess" being thrown around among my friends whenever Hazel was around, but I'd never called her that. I'd called her something she'd disliked a lot more.

Without acknowledging the truth behind my dad's statement, I said goodbye and got out of here. I had a job to do.

When I got to the bookstore, I stood outside, watching Hazel Riley move around like a fucking creeper.

What kind of man was I if I lurked in the shadows instead of walking in there to approach her? Sure as hell seemed like I was afraid of her, but that wasn't quite it. Regret, maybe?

Fuck. We'd gone to high school together, for god's sake, and had barely spoken. Though the times we had hadn't been all that positive. They'd been bad. If I walked in there, I was likely to catch a book to the head and Hazel would make sure it was the thickest in the store. Whatever would do the most damage.

Inside, I prayed to the universe that she didn't remember anything that had happened back then.

Hazel caught my eye as I paced in front of the store. She was on her knees on the floor, stacking some books. She'd look at the spine of a book, then place it in a certain pile. Look at another and place it in the other pile. She repeated this over and over, oblivious to the fact that I was out there, which meant she would've been oblivious to anyone else as well.

That didn't sit right with me. One thing Dad had drilled into me from a young age was to protect those you cared about as well as anyone who might've needed it.

Damn. She was just as beautiful as she'd been in high school. That rich, red hair that always looked so soft, though I'd never had the opportunity to discover if it was or not. Hazel Riley wouldn't have given me a chance in high school or a second look.

Which was how I found myself outside of this bookstore trying to get my courage up to go in and face her, knowing that an apology was going to come sooner or later. It wasn't my favorite thing to do.

After two quick breaths, I pushed through the door before I could talk myself out of it. I'd been standing out there so long, she'd probably finished with the books.

"Welcome to Pick-a-Book. Can I h—" Her words cut off when she came around the corner and saw me standing there with my hands hanging limply at my sides and my jaw tight as I prepared for whatever reaction she was going to give me.

Damn. She was still beautiful with those red curls and green eyes I'd swear had been cut from jade. This was going to be harder than I'd thought. Her eyes hardened like green steel, if there was such a thing, and that ever-present smile from high school that I saw when she was with her friends and didn't know I was watching, was nowhere to be found.

Yup. She remembered me. Hopefully, she also remembered that all of the cause for that anger was mostly not my doing. Fucking Oliver had done most of the teasing, I'd thought to overcompensate for his pining over a girl who he'd never named. But whatever.

"Hey, Hazel. How ya doing?" I jammed my hands into my pockets and smiled.

She rolled her eyes, but it hadn't escaped my notice that when she'd first seen me, her eyes had scanned from head to toe. "What are you doing here, Miller?"

"Maybe I'm looking for a book." I lifted my arms in the air to indicate all of the books around us. "We *are* in a bookstore."

She cocked her head to the side and snorted. "Have you ever been in a bookstore before?"

I clutched my chest roughly where I thought my heart was. "I'm wounded. You don't think I can read?"

"I know you can read." Her eyes narrowed on me before she turned her back to me and walked toward the cash register. "If you couldn't read, then you wouldn't have been able to write those things about me in the boys' bathroom, now would you have?"

A brick dropped in my stomach. I'd hoped she'd never heard about that, but it hadn't been me. Luken, Oliver, and I had spent days trying to find out who it had been. When we had, we'd made sure he wouldn't do it again.

"That wasn't me." Though it made sense that she thought it was.

She sighed. "Sure, it wasn't." Then she finally looked up at me again. "So what book are you looking for?" she asked, her eyes settled on mine again.

Having Hazel so close caused a tightness in my chest. Some might've called it nervousness, but I didn't get nervous around women and hadn't since I'd been a junior in high school and this fiery redhead would float on by acting like she couldn't be bothered with most of us.

"Huh?" I asked.

Hazel wasn't big by any means. She was over half a foot shorter than me with curves in all the right places. And right now, she reminded me of an angry chihuahua. Ready to strike out to sink her teeth into my ankle at any moment. When she let out a long, frustrated sigh, I felt that in my chest too.

"A book, Miller. A book. You're in a bookstore and said that maybe you came for a book," she said. I was still focused on the way her lips formed my name when she snapped her fingers in front of me. "If you're not here for a book, then what *are* you here for and how do I get you to leave?"

"I'm here to ask you out for coffee."

Her stern face cracked as a loud laugh burst up from her chest. I don't think I'd ever asked a woman out only to have her laugh in my face before. Sure, I'd been turned down and all of that, but this... It was different and it took everything in me not to laugh right along with her. The sound of her laughter was contagious, but the situation was ridiculous.

Mostly, I focused on the way her lips curved into a smile. I hadn't seen much of that up close.

"Oh, come on," she said once she'd gotten herself back under control. Yes, she was still laughing, but at least she could talk again.

"Come on what?"

Her hand was bracing her side. "I haven't laughed that hard since..." She blinked five times thinking about it. "I don't think I've ever laughed that hard in my entire life. What are you up to, Miller? Did you miss harassing me these last three years because, to be honest, I haven't missed you." She wet her lips quickly. "Or thought about you in any way. So fess up."

I didn't want to admit, least of all to myself, how her saying she hadn't thought of me in three years burned a hole in my chest. *Fuck.*

We hadn't been that bad, had we?

It hadn't even really been me. There'd been a group of guys who'd called her "princess" and tormented her over the fact that her family had money and she hung around the rich kids, which automatically, to us at the time, meant she'd thought she was better than the rest of us.

Even with Oliver giving her shit sometimes, when the really bad things happened, like the disgusting things written on the bathroom wall, we'd found the guy and taken care of it, much the way we did with basically any guy who showed even the tiniest interest in the girl Oliver had injured when we'd been kids. It'd been an accident but she hated his ass after that.

"Look." I placed my hands on the counter and leaned in until we were close enough that she'd feel my breath on her face. Her mouth dropped open and her breathing increased. "I'm sorry for any of the incredibly stupid things I did in high school. I don't know what to say to explain it, but I was clearly an asshole and obviously immature—"

"Not to mention a dick."

I snorted. "Wouldn't that be covered under being an asshole?"

"No." She shook her head emphatically. "Those are two completely different categories."

"OK. And being a dick. I'm sorry," I said. Her gaze dropped to my mouth when I licked my bottom lip. "What's it going to take to get you to go get coffee with me?"

"I don't know," she whispered. Then she took a giant step back, like being too close to me hindered her ability to think straight, and damn, I hoped it did because being this close to her, smelling the vanilla lotion on her skin, had me not thinking all that clearly myself.

"You don't know?"

"Yeah." She held her arms listlessly next to her body. "I don't know. You were really mean to me for years and I'm supposed to believe that you one day, you were like, 'Huh. Wonder what Hazel's doing. I should go see if she wants coffee?'" She shook her head again then slid out from behind the counter and pretended to straighten the stuffed animals on the nearest shelf. "I don't buy it."

"You don't buy which part?" I asked, following her around like a lost puppy.

"All of it. The fact that you're even in this store, but specifically, the apology you just gave. I don't buy it."

Against my better judgment, my hand shot out and grabbed her arm to stop her pointless movement around the store. She was just doing it to avoid having to look at me. Even I could read that.

Once she was facing me, I said, "I *am* sorry, Hazel. For any grief I gave you in high school or any problems you had because of me." Then I swallowed hard. "I promise if you saw Oliver, he'd say it too."

"Yeah, somehow Luken was the only one that didn't give me any trouble. Why was that?"

I groaned and ran my hand down my face. "I don't know, but please remember things clearly. I didn't do anything to you."

"You called me 'cupcake' for two years. I hated it and you knew I hated it." She sighed and threw her hands up in the air. "I didn't think I was better than any of you, which was something I was accused of all the time."

"I know." I nodded though her hating the nickname was the exact reason I used it. Hazel's irritation was adorable. Like an angry teacup puppy. "We were idiots. Please tell me what I can do to get you to go to coffee with me. We can talk everything out and you'll see that I am sorry."

Hazel sucked her bottom lip into her mouth. I could just barely see her teeth digging into it. My biggest hope was that she was thinking about it. To keep from failing the coven I needed her to say *yes*. It was the only way to break the ice.

"Are you saying that you'll do whatever I ask to get me to say *yes* to coffee?" Her red, wavy hair fell like a curtain when she cocked her head to the side.

That hair had been how I could pick her out of a crowd in school. She'd been too short for me to see her, but that hair... couldn't be missed. I'd had an affinity for redheads ever since.

"Yes." I'd wanted to add "within reason," but there was nothing she could ask that I wouldn't do because I had no choice. I had to get her to trust me.

She tapped her index finger against her chin. This was the perfect chance for her to get whatever payback against me that she wanted. I'd have to endure whatever came out of her mouth next.

"I know!" Her eyes widened in enjoyment as she

tried to smother a smile. "I know what you could do."

"Name it."

She hurried away from me. I followed because what else was I going to do? Hazel was on the move until she suddenly came to a stop. She spun around with a book in her hand.

"What's this?" I asked.

The smile on her face made me uncomfortable, but she pushed the book into my hands anyway. "Read this."

"Read this?"

"Yeah. This is the last thing that I read that I really loved. Read that and then we'll talk."

"Are you serious right now?"

"Very. I assume it'll be a while before I see you again." She patted me on the back three times before leaving me standing there with a book in my hand. "Why don't you text me when you finish and we'll meet for coffee then?"

"Sounds good, but I'll need your phone number to do that."

She sighed and held out her hand. After unlocking my phone, I handed it over to her and watched as she tapped her information into my phone.

I supposed I was spending the night reading... what looked like a paranormal romance. I'd never read a romance before and that was likely why she'd chosen it.

If that was what I had to do to get Hazel to give me a chance, then that was what I'd have to do.

I couldn't fail at this.

4
———

HAZEL

Giving Miller Campbell that book had been the easiest way to get out of going to coffee with him. He hadn't been terrible at school, but he hadn't been known for reading romance for pleasure. There was no way he was going to go through with it and I was off the hook. And yes, I knew that just saying *no* should've been enough, but this was easier.

Whatever his motives, I assumed he'd take the book, which he'd paid for, and I'd never hear from him again. But around ten the next morning, I received a text asking me when I'd like to meet for coffee.

What the hell? Leave it to Miller to do the opposite of what I'd expected.

Are you saying that you already read the whole book?

His reply was instant. *Yup.*

Seriously?

Yup.

Damn, his one-word answers weren't giving me much. But I'd given my word that if he read the book, I'd meet him for coffee. What if he hadn't? He could've said he'd read it and totally not. Clearly, he needed a test.

How about eleven? I work at one and I swear if you didn't read the book… Well, I don't know what I'll do, but you better have read the book.

Lol, Hazel. I read the book. I'll meet you at eleven at Perk Up.

Our town was basically famous for the kitschy names of our businesses and I thought that was half the draw.

After that text from Miller this morning, I didn't want to admit to myself that I put extra time into getting ready when I shouldn't have. This was Miller. A guy from high school who hadn't liked me then and I'd assumed still didn't. Though why would he ask me out then?

Didn't matter.

Honestly, I didn't like him, either, though even I

couldn't deny how incredibly hot he was. That messy, blond hair and those clear, blue eyes had made all the girls swoon back then. Probably still did.

I arrived at the coffee shop way too early but told myself it was absolutely not because I was nervous or excited. Neither of those feelings was something I could admit to myself or anyone else. Only teenage me knew that he'd made my heart beat faster whenever he'd pass me in the hall. Only teenage me got to remember that I'd had to work hard not to blush when he'd sat near me in the cafeteria.

It had been a hard two years.

Instead, I'd perpetuated the lie that it was because I was a habitually early person. Well, it wasn't a lie, exactly, because I did tend to show up to everything early, but that wasn't the sole reason this time.

To make it seem normal, I ordered coffee and grabbed a table by the window. The iced mocha latte tasted like heaven and would give me something to do with my hands when he showed up.

Much to my surprise, Miller walked through the door early as well.

"You already ordered," he said when he came to a stop beside my table.

Unfortunately, I'd just taken a drink and my mouth was full. The harder I tried to swallow, the more difficult it became. "I did," I finally choked out once the drink was down.

"I invited you, Hazel. Tradition says I'm supposed to pay."

"Well, I was early and thirsty. We could argue about it or—"

He sighed and the mere act of raising his hand cut me off. "Let me go grab something. I'll be right back."

Miller sauntered over to the counter to place his order. The young woman working today, whom I didn't recognize when she'd taken my order and I hadn't even looked at her name tag, giggled as he spoke. She leaned in closer to him as he kept his voice down, which meant I couldn't hear them.

Their interaction told me that they already knew each other, but just how well wasn't clear. Watching the two of them made me squirm in my seat, like I was intruding on a personal moment.

Then she laughed. It was a full-of-life kind of thing before she playfully slapped Miller's arm and stepped away. He came back to me once she'd gone to work on his drink.

"You're a flirt," I told him once he'd sat across

from me. "I knew you were in high school. I just didn't know you still are." It shouldn't have bothered me as much as it did. Miller was free to do whatever he wanted and I shouldn't have cared.

"Yeah. Sorry." He scrubbed his hand over his chin. "It's kind of second nature. I wasn't trying to flirt with her."

I was sure it was second nature for him. With everyone but me. "It was an observation. Nothing more. You can flirt with whomever you want. Not like this is a date."

His jaw tensed. "No. It isn't. If it were, I'd be more careful. I promise."

"Good to know," I said. His gaze was so intense that I shifted in my seat. He wasn't going to get the best of me. I didn't care that it felt like he was touching me when he was only looking. "So... the book?"

Miller smothered a smile and then opened his mouth to respond, but the barista called his name. He held up a finger to tell me to wait, grabbed his coffee, then was back and ready to go again.

"The book." He took a drink of his coffee. I had no idea what was inside the cup, other than it was hot rather than cold. "It was good."

I raised an eyebrow, which just made him laugh.

"You don't think I read it, do you?" he asked.

No reason not to be honest. "No. I don't."

His brow tilted down as he leaned forward, setting his arms on the table, one folded on top of the other. "I'm not lying."

"Then prove it."

"Prove that I read the book?"

"Yes."

He took another long, slow drink. "Why don't you believe me and how would I prove it?"

I leaned up to mimic how he was sitting to prove he wasn't intimidating me, even though deep down, he kind of was. Because Miller was beautiful up close, even when he'd been a dick to me. "I don't believe you read it because I just gave it to you yesterday."

He shrugged. "I'm a fast reader. So how do I prove it?"

"Easy," I told him. "Tell me your favorite part."

He snorted then said, "You could've asked something a little harder. The sex was my favorite part."

I closed my eyes and shook my head. Yeah, I'd walked into that one. The coffee shop began to fill with people. Not too crowded and we already had a table anyway, but the chatter helped put me at ease. "Of course. Can you be more specific?"

One corner of his mouth turned up, making him look as cocky as he'd always acted. cockier than he normally was. "You want me to be more specific about the sex that I liked?"

My cheeks burned as I slapped a hand over my face. "What? No."

"You asked."

"Miller." I sighed as I removed my hand. "Tell me something about the book that makes me believe you read it because if you tricked—"

"I don't trick people, Hazel. I read the fucking book." He sat back in his chair, his gaze still on me, but I wouldn't give him the satisfaction of breaking the connection. He wasn't scaring me away. "OK. My favorite sex scene was the one in the truck, but the fact that I know that Kieran was just trying to keep Stella and Tomas apart because he wanted her for himself, not because he loved her, but because he didn't like to lose should be enough to tell you I read the book."

My lips parted in surprise and my eyes widened. He'd actually read it. To get me to have coffee with him. None of this made sense.

"Is that enough?" he asked.

To cover my surprise, I grabbed my coffee and took a nice, long drink.

But this was Miller. The same guy I'd known in high school. The same guy who'd stood by while his friends treated me like garbage... OK maybe not like garbage, but not good. They'd said things and called me "princess" because my parents had money when I'd just tried to be a good person. And I supposed they weren't all his friends. Oliver was and did those things, though Luken didn't as much.

The way Miller had called me "cupcake" for two years on those rare times we'd had interactions had been so much worse than being called "princess." My friend Lindsay had tried to tell me once that him doing it bothered me more because I'd had a crush on him. She'd been immediately refuted as I'd insisted that he'd revolted me. She'd only proclaimed I'd protested too much. No winning.

"OK. So what do you want?" I finally asked him.

"What do you mean?"

I tilted my head to the side and narrowed my eyes. He couldn't be serious. "Miller. You walk into the store where I have worked for years, one I'd guess you've never been in before, and ask me to coffee. You have to want something from me."

His gaze dropped from my eyes to my mouth and then back again, causing a stirring low in my stomach. I couldn't let this guy affect me. That was when

I'd let my guard down and I wasn't doing that with Miller Campbell.

"What do you want, Miller?" I repeated. "I know this isn't just a social call because guys like you aren't interested in women like me. So just tell me."

He furrowed his brows. "Explain please."

"Which part?"

"Guys like me. Women like you." He twirled his finger in the air. "Explain."

Sometimes I wished I had better control of the word vomit that randomly fell from my mouth. I took a deep breath. "You know what I mean, Miller. You're..." I waved my hand in front of him as I said, "You. You're you and I'm me."

"Again, explain please."

I rolled my eyes and groaned. There was no way to explain this without sounding like I was putting myself down. I wasn't. My confidence was fine, but the fact remained that he preferred the obviously gorgeous women who could have casual sex without looking back. There was nothing wrong with that. I just wasn't part of that group. "You could probably go out and get any woman you want. Don't try to deny it."

He chuckled. "I wasn't going to."

"Yet you're here in this coffee shop with a woman

you couldn't stand in high school, one who reads romance novels, sometimes trashy ones. A woman who—"

"It doesn't matter." He settled his arms on the table again. "What did I do to you in high school? Because I'm trying to remember and not coming up with much."

Again, he wasn't exactly wrong. He hadn't personally done much of anything for the most part, but the people around him had. "You didn't stop your friends from being assholes."

"I don't control them."

"You called me 'cupcake' knowing that I hated it."

"Isn't that the equivalent of a boy pulling a girl's hair for attention?"

"That's not something girls should be taught means a boy likes them. That's dangerous and ends up with women thinking it's fine to be treated like trash."

"I didn't treat you like trash." He moved his coffee cup slowly in a circle while thinking about what he wanted to say next. "I'm sorry I called you 'cupcake' knowing that it bothered you. Clearly, it bugged you even more than I realized. Otherwise, you wouldn't have mentioned it." His tongue slid over his bottom lip. "I could tell you it's because I thought you'd taste sweet like frosting, which you probably do, but back then, I was just a hormonal guy thinking with his dick more than anything else." His eyes finally settled on mine again. "And *that* guy, I wouldn't let near you."

All I could do was blink and try to process what Miller had just said. Putting aside that he'd literally told me he thought I'd taste like frosting and that was inherently sexual by anyone's measure. On top of that, he'd admitted to how he'd been in high school.

I still didn't know if I believed him or not, but he'd been committed enough to read that whole book last night. That had to mean something.

One thing was for certain: I wouldn't let him know that I felt that way. I'd still be on guard in case this was some elaborate joke of his. Though he hadn't done anything to make me think that.

"Then why are we here?" I asked him. At this point, I really wished that he was easier to read because right now, I was getting nothing off him when in reality, most of the time I at least had a sense of where someone was headed.

"I was walking by the store and saw you in there picking up books that were on the floor and I knew I had to talk to you. Had to ask you to come here." He leaned in again. "I'm really hoping you're not regretting it."

"I'm not," I said too quickly. Then I sighed and decided to be completely honest with him. "It's just weird for me. I have my friends, I have people whom I talk to, but you've never been in that group. Now here we are having coffee."

"Don't friends get coffee?"

"That's the thing, Miller. We're not friends."

"Maybe I want to be." Miller took a quick drink and averted his gaze out the window, avoiding my eyes the way some people did when they were either lying or they were admitting to something they didn't necessarily want to admit to. "Maybe I wanted to be in high school."

Now I laughed. "Sure, you did. If you wanted to be friends in high school, nothing was stopping you."

"*You* stopped me," he said louder than I thought he meant to. Loud enough for several people around us to turn our way.

The strong aroma of coffee in the air was like the best candle that had ever been lit. There were more people in the place, which meant more coffee being made, which resulted in the strong smell. I wouldn't knock it.

"*I* stopped you?" I asked because I wasn't so full of myself to believe that I'd never done anything wrong. I'd wronged people. Everyone has, but I wanted to know what, specifically, he was talking about because even back then, Miller had been the best-looking guy I'd ever seen. If I'd been doing something to chase him off, then whom else had I done that to?

"Well, not you exactly," he corrected. "The idea of you, Hazel. You were always so confident. You walked around like nothing anyone said bothered you. Plus, you were hot as hell even back then. You were intimidating."

I was intimidating? He had to be messing with me, right? Miller could've had anyone he'd wanted back then, including me, and from what I could tell, he'd used that to his advantage. None of this was making sense.

When I glanced at the clock, I realized that I needed to get moving. We'd been here longer than I'd intended to be and I had another errand to run before work.

"Well, I'm sorry I intimidated you, though that's rather hard for me to believe," I said. He reached out and pushed a piece of hair back behind my ear. My entire body froze when his thumb brushed against my cheek. "I have to go." The words fell out of my mouth as if I were worried I wouldn't have time to say them.

"Work?"

"Yeah." I nodded. "And I have an errand to run." It was just to the bank and the store quickly, but I didn't want to give him that information. What if he offered to go with me? I didn't think I could take much more Miller right now.

I needed space. I needed air to breathe.

"Yeah. I should get to work too."

He stood first, taking both his coffee cup and mine with him. I'd sucked mine dry at least fifteen minutes ago. Then he dropped them into the trash can nearest us.

We walked out together as I prayed none of my friends would see me with him.

"It was..." I grappled with my thoughts, trying to find the right word as we stood out in front of the coffee shop for this incredibly awkward goodbye. "Nice. It was nice to see you, Miller, even if I still don't fully understand the reason."

"It was good seeing you too, Hazel." The humor dancing on his lips, begging to be let out, had better stay held back or I was going to... Well, I didn't know what I was going to do, but something. "Since this went so well and neither of us killed the other, how about we get dinner tonight? Are you free? What time do you get off work?"

My mind was spinning as that pesky tingling radiated up from my lady bits. Stupid hormones. I couldn't even count the number of times that I'd thought about Miller at night when I... Nope. Not going there.

"Dinner? Tonight?" I stammered out.

"Yeah. What time are you done?"

"I'm done at six-thirty."

"How about seven, then? I can pick you up."

"No." My eyes were so wide that I couldn't imagine what I looked like, but I couldn't have him pick me up from my house. I couldn't be trapped in a car with him for any length of time. Not yet.

He cocked his head to the side. "No to dinner or no to picking you up?"

"Picking me up. I'll meet you wherever you want. Just text me."

"OK. I'll see you then, Hazel." He began to walk away while I just stood there like an idiot. "Oh, and Hazel," he called out. "I'll be paying, so please don't order and pay if you beat me there."

I snorted because that sounded like something I'd do, but I shook my head and gave him the finger.

People in high school might've seen me as a priss when in reality, I'd been anything but.

Ohmygod.

I'd basically just agreed to a date with Miller Campbell. What the hell was wrong with me?

5

HAZEL

THE HOURS AT WORK WENT BY SLOWER THAN molasses in January, as my grandmother used to say. It meant really slowly, but I liked the colorful visuals that she always used in describing anything. It just made things better.

Our little bookstore had so many people packed into it that they were tripping over each other, but luckily, they'd just laugh and move on. The smell of books put people in a good mood and summer brought even more people from the city to Echo Valley.

I pulled my hair back into a ponytail because I was getting so warm and we turned down the thermostat so the air conditioning would run more often. Books couldn't cover body odor.

Finally, around three-thirty, I took a break.

After grabbing a bottle of water from the fridge in the break room, I pulled my phone out of my back pocket to call my best friend, Lindsay. She wasn't going to believe that I'd had coffee with Miller today or anything that had come after.

But maybe, just maybe, she'd help me parse out his ulterior motive because there had to be one.

"Are you working?" she asked into the phone without a greeting. She knew my schedule, though we hadn't talked in over a week since she was on vacation and didn't always get great reception in parts of Europe.

I wasn't jealous at all.

Her father didn't mind funding her exploits while mine would add conditions that included going to his stupid fundraisers and I wouldn't give him the satisfaction.

"I am, but I'm on break and have something to tell you that you're not going to believe." The words rushed out of my mouth again.

"Please don't tell me that you're pregnant."

"Ew. No. Why do people always guess that when a woman has news?"

Not to mention that my vagina had an overgrowth of webs since it'd been quite a long time since anyone had been down there. I'd broken up with my last boyfriend the previous summer and there hadn't been anyone else since.

The mere thought of sex brought with it images of Miller that I had to push away from my sanity.

"Well... what am I supposed to believe when you tell me you have big news?"

"I didn't—never mind. I don't have time to argue that." I dropped into a seat at the tiny bistro table we had in the breakroom. "You're not going to believe who came into the store yesterday and asked me to coffee today and read *Lonely Witches* last night just to prove that he wanted to see me today?"

Silence met me from the other line. "That was... a lot. And very specific."

I snickered. She wasn't wrong. "Miller Campbell." She was never going to guess anyway.

"Shut. Up." All of the noise behind her had died out, as if she'd moved to a quieter area. Man, I should've Facetimed her just so I could live vicariously and see her face at this new information, though I could've pictured it just as well.

Her dark hair was tied up in a bun and her darker skin tone was tanned from all of her time outside. Then when she'd heard what I'd said, her mouth had dropped open, even though she was trying not to smile and her eyes were wide. Or that was what it looked like in my head.

"I know, right? It was so weird to see him standing there in the store yesterday."

"Now why did he read the book, though? And what did he want?"

"He read the book because I told him it was the only way to prove that he wanted to meet me for coffee. I had to think of something." I shrugged, still kind of proud of myself for that one. "And apparently, he just wanted to talk. He apologized for being a dick in high school."

"He wasn't that bad," she countered.

Lindsay had never once hidden how hot she'd found Miller, nor how she'd have been up for just about anything if he would've asked her out. He never had. Not once, even though I knew for a fact that she'd offered on more than one occasion.

"I know." I sighed. Her defending him wasn't new, either. "But we went to coffee today. Talked a little and he asked me to dinner tonight."

"Shut. Up," she repeated. "Are you fucking with me right now?"

"I am not. The coffee went fine and he asked me to dinner. Tonight."

"You said *yes*, right?"

I bit my lips together briefly before answering her. "I did, but I don't know why. You were the one with a crush on him in high school." I shook my head as I kept the lie of me being indifferent to Miller in place. "I don't know why I said *yes*. Though I did think quickly enough to say that I'd meet him so I'm not cooped up in a car with him. Could you imagine?"

"Yeah, I could." She sounded almost wistful.

"Wait. Lindsay, it's OK I said *yes*, right? I mean I don't think it's a date or anything, but if you don't want—"

Now her loud laughter cut me off. "Stop it. I was kidding. Miller Campbell is nothing more than a memory for me. But, Hazel, this absolutely is a date. There's no question. What are you going to wear?"

My stomach clenched and a nervous fluttering butterfly flapped its wings in my stomach.

A date?

It couldn't be a date.

This was Miller Campbell for crying out loud.

Shit. This was a date.

I looked down at myself. The clothes I was

wearing to work were cute but not exactly *date night* appropriate. "I'm not sure, but I've got to get back to work."

"We'll talk soon."

I ended the call, downed almost the entire bottle of water, then headed back out to the front.

The rest of the day, I obsessed over my options for tonight. When he'd said he'd pick me up at seven and I'd countered with meeting him, I'd assumed I'd just wear what I was wearing now. But after talking to Lindsay, I was thinking that wasn't the best idea ever.

The universe was smiling upon me when Dad sent a text saying they had a function tonight and I was on my own for dinner. What was he talking about? I was on my own most nights because I chose to be. Hanging out with them didn't exactly fill me with joy.

He probably thought he was being sneaky or making me jealous over their glamorous lifestyle and all the while, I couldn't care less.

But with them gone, I could go home, change my clothes, and ask Miller to pick me up there. This was Echo Valley, after all, and my fear of being stuck with him if he drove was quashed by the fact that I could walk home if I had to. Plus, I wouldn't be late and I'd get to put on a new outfit and maybe smack some makeup over my face.

It was the perfect plan.

On my next slow moment, I shot off a text to Miller asking if he'd mind my new plan. He replied right away that he'd be there at seven.

It didn't take long to settle on what I was going to wear. My new white dress, for sure. It went so well with my slightly tanned summer skin. I didn't tan, exactly. Mostly I just burned because of being a ginger. However, I did obtain a healthy glow in the sun.

"Today was busy," my co-worker Emmi said as we got to the end of my shift and the store had mostly cleared out. Emmi had this beautiful brown hair that hung almost to her waist and that she tended to keep in a long braid.

It was one of those lulls we got during the day that we appreciated more than anything. That was the great thing about being busy. You appreciated when you weren't instead of complaining when things were slow.

"Yeah, it was." I sighed. "I'm so glad I'm almost done."

"Lucky. I'm closing." But she'd also come in after me. "Got any big Saturday night plans?"

My stomach lurched. Did I want to tell anyone else that I was going out with Miller? Not really, but I also couldn't ignore her question and saw no reason to lie. "I'm just going to dinner with a guy from high school."

Her eyes widened and danced with excitement. "Oh, really? Anybody, I'd know?"

Emmi was a few years older than Miller, but it was entirely possible that she'd know who he was. Still, I didn't want to tell her because if this whole thing blew up in my face, I'd prefer to limit my embarrassment.

"I don't think so," I said quickly. She and I walked to the back of the store to the breakroom. It also happened to be where we kept our personal belongings when we came to work. I grabbed my purse from the cubby I used and said, "You have a good night."

"You too." As I walked away, she added, "I want to hear all about it."

Yeah. That probably wasn't going to happen.

When I got home, I kicked it into high gear. I only had twenty minutes to do everything I wanted to. If Miller wasn't early. I didn't know him well enough to predict whether he was a punctual person or tended to run late, other than at the coffee shop.

First, I stripped down and did a quick washing up, hitting all the important places. Running around the store had gotten me sweaty, especially when we'd been busy. Then I brushed out my hair and bent some waves into it. I didn't intend to do anything overly fancy, given my limited time. Then I brushed some mascara over my lashes and swiped on some lip gloss.

Once that was taken care of, I pulled my new white sundress out of the closet and hurriedly yanked it on.

I'd loved this thing when I'd bought it. It had spaghetti straps, which meant I had to ditch my bra, but the cups of the bodice made my breasts look fantastic, even if not as perky as when I was wearing a bra. They came together in a V just above my diaphragm. The top had an almost crocheted effect, a thick ruching at the waist, and a flowy skirt.

It was perfect.

I'd just slid on the cute sandals that I'd bought to go along with this dress when our doorbell rang. The shoes were flat and didn't have much to them, but the thong between my toes rose up into a sparkly strap that kept the shoes on my feet.

I hit every light switch on the way downstairs and yanked open the front door.

Miller stood before me in jeans and a blue short-sleeved button-down shirt that made his eyes look dangerously sexy and almost unreal.

"Hey," he said with a panty-melting smile.

Damn this guy for looking so good.

"Hi. I'm ready to go." I pushed out the door and pulled it shut behind me.

Miller snickered. "Don't want the parents to meet me?"

"They're not even here." I stopped when I came to his black Challenger. It was the same car he'd driven when he'd been a senior and I kind of hated remembering that.

After taking a minute to regain my thoughts, I got moving again and slid into the butter-soft leather seats. Normally, I wasn't a fan of leather seats, but this car was vintage and I remembered hearing that he'd rebuilt it with Oliver and Luken. The three of them must've been really good with their hands.

Shaking off that last thought, I asked, "So where are we going?"

"I was going to text you earlier and unless you have another idea, I'm thinking we get dinner at The Cave. It's not the—"

"Perfect. They have the best burgers. And their

nachos." I put my fingers to my lips in a chef's kiss. "Delicious."

Miller chuckled. "Everything there is so good."

I'd cut him off because it seemed like he'd been going to say it wasn't the fanciest place or whatever and it wasn't, which was why it was my favorite.

Growing up with money, people always assumed that I preferred expensive things, but it wasn't even close to that. I was like everyone else.

The two of us made small talk on the drive to the restaurant. Talking about work seemed like a safe enough topic. He'd spent his day working on a car that was giving him a lot of trouble, but since I didn't understand cars further than putting the key in to start it, most of what he said didn't make sense.

But I could listen to him talk about anything.

The Cave was a bar and grill, which meant on a Saturday night, it was crowded. It was also a popular choice for locals, which I didn't remember until we stepped inside and noticed the number of eyes on us.

Miller settled his hand on my lower back to lead me to an empty booth in the corner. His hand scorched my skin through the thin fabric of my dress and the heat spread throughout my body, settling any nerves that had popped up.

It was like his touch was magic.

At least ten people said *hello* to him as we passed, which didn't surprise me. Echo Valley wasn't big and Miller had known everyone in high school. Working at the garage, he'd probably met the ones since that he hadn't already known back then.

If people would've thought about it, they would've recognized me too. I just kept a much lower profile and spent a lot of time outside of Echo Valley at school, so it wasn't obvious to them.

Once we were settled, the waitress came for our drink order, but we put in our food order at the same time. There was no reason to peruse the menu for ten minutes when we both already knew what we wanted.

"That dress is something else," he said after our drinks were dropped off. I'd asked for a water and he'd ordered a pop.

I looked down at myself and then back to him. "Something good or something bad? That's a vague way to describe it."

Miller chuckled as he ran his hand over his chin and then the back of his head like I'd made him uncomfortable.

"Definitely something good."

"Thank you." My cheeks burned, but I ignored

that. There was no chance I made him as uncomfortable as he made me.

Just being near Miller again made me ache and I pressed my thighs together to appease the sensation. Didn't work, but that crush I'd had a million years ago seemed to be a thing lingering inside of me.

Spending time with him as friends was going to be difficult on my end. If that was what we were doing. I was still suspicious.

"So you've been working at the garage since you graduated?" I asked him.

"Pretty much. I love it there, though, and both Oliver and Luken work at the same place, so it's a lot of fun. I always know that whatever the problem is with a car, I'll be able to fix it, even if it takes a while."

"You like fixing problems?" That question sounded like I was trying to psychoanalyze him. I wasn't, exactly. I was just trying to get to know him again, though it felt like no time had passed. The limited interactions we'd had in high school were still so fresh in my brain.

"I like it when it's a problem I can fix."

There was so much to unpack from that statement that I didn't know where to start. Realistically, it would probably be better if I just kept my mouth shut on that one. Though I couldn't help wondering what kind of problems he had that he couldn't fix because from where I was sitting, Miller had it all together.

As far as I could tell, there wasn't much Miller couldn't fix.

6

———

MILLER

Sitting across the table from Hazel was surreal. Her powers simmered under the surface and I wondered why I'd never noticed them before. More than that, I was curious as to how *she* didn't feel them. My powers felt like a warm liquid flooding my body that couldn't be ignored. Of course, I'd been trained in how to harness them.

I'd thought about Hazel many times in the three years since I'd graduated and maybe I'd kept my eye out for her around town, yet I never really saw her. Odd, considering that she worked at the bookstore and probably had friends who worked here.

Then I remembered that she'd been on a different track than me in school.

"You're in college, right?" I asked.

"I go to Huron State," she told me before taking a quick drink of her water. "My parents preferred it and since they're paying... Anyway, I live with them but spend most of my time in the city."

"Except for in the summer?"

She nodded. "Except for in the summer."

Our waitress dropped our food off and told us to let her know if we needed anything else before she left us alone again.

"How do you like it?" I asked her then took a big bite of my burger.

"School? I love it. Mostly because it's going to help get me out of my parents' house. I'm majoring in business so hopefully that will help me get a job."

My jaw hardened. "You don't like it there." It wasn't a question, but a statement.

"No. I don't." I noticed that she stopped eating and her hands fell into her lap. "I know everyone thinks that because my father has money that things are just golden with me. And that's not the case. I have the same problems as everyone else and incredibly high parental expectations."

"What kind of expectations?"

"They keep wanting me to go to these fundraisers with them."

"Fundraisers?" That was bullshit and I already

knew it. I would've bet my left nut that those *fundraisers* were a cover for the shadow coven. I wasn't sure how I knew, but I did and now it made even more sense as to why Michael wanted someone to bring Hazel to our side.

In the battle between the light and the dark, a choice had to be made. I'd been told that about a million times since I'd been a kid. It was always a choice, but the shadow coven sometimes tricked witches into making that choice, whereas the light did not.

"Yeah." She shook her head and then began to pick at her food again. "I have no idea what they're for, but they always want me to go and try to sway me by saying there'll be eligible guys will be there. It's disgusting."

"They want you to find an appropriate boyfriend?" I fucking hated that like hell.

She shrugged. "I guess. But there's zero chance I'd like anyone they did, so I've never worried about it."

The idea of Hazel with anyone else hit me like a punch to the chest. It always had. She'd gone to my senior prom with Micha Anderson. He'd been a senior when she'd been a sophomore and I'd had a lot less fun watching his hands on her that night.

If Hazel ever knew the kinds of thoughts I'd had about her back then... I wasn't entirely sure she'd believe me. Especially since she thought very different kinds of things about me.

"Do me a favor," I told her, knowing that I would be walking a fine line between teaching without influencing her as we were supposed to do and totally influencing her. "Don't go to any of your parents' fundraisers."

Hazel snorted then popped a fry into her mouth. "You don't have to worry about that at all. I have no intention of ever going."

That was at least a relief.

As we talked, I realized how much I had to hold back. I couldn't even accidentally let any of the coven work slip. She wasn't ready to hear that she was a witch. Instead, I focused on work and some of the dumber things Luken, Oliver, and I had done over the years. Though her eyes darkened every time I mentioned Oliver, and I began to wonder if he'd done more to her than I'd known.

Hazel even asked me about the women I'd dated, but I most certainly didn't want to talk about that. Not with her.

Once we'd finished, I paid and then drove back

to her house. We'd had such a good time that I didn't want to let her go. Alas, I had to.

"Are you in a hurry to get home?" she asked after I pulled into her driveway.

"No." My answer was automatic. The last thing I wanted to do at this point was leave her.

Part of it was the crush I'd had on her all those years ago and the fact that it hadn't gone away. If we would've talked like this in high school, it would've been a totally different story.

"Then come on." Hazel hopped out of my car and headed toward the back of her house.

The Rileys' house was huge compared to any of the houses I knew of. Which was probably why they lived outside of town on a good amount of land. It was two stories and probably had lots of rooms.

I followed Hazel around. My steps faltered right before I caught up to her. The back of this place was amazing. There was a walkway that headed out into the darkness. Who knew how far this went, but the sides were dotted with solar lights that illuminated the path. In the distance was a pond. Not overly huge, but a pond nonetheless with a dock that looked like one of those detachable ones that would float out into the water.

They also had a pool and when I saw it, my mind

immediately went to Hazel in a bikini. My hands itched to make contact with the silky-looking skin on her back. This dress should've been illegal.

Hazel tossed her purse onto a table and waved me on.

"What're we doing back here?" I asked quietly once I was beside her. Part of me was hoping she was going to say skinny-dipping, but I didn't think we were there yet.

"Walking." She glanced at me then away. "Unless you don't want to. I just wasn't ready to go inside yet."

"Your parents are home?"

She shook her head. "They'll be late, but the house still feels claustrophobic even when they're not here."

This house was big enough that I knew space wasn't the issue. "Well, I've got all night."

A smile appeared, but it was small and not all that joyful. "What's going on?" I asked as I brushed her hair back over her shoulder. When she didn't flinch, I took it as a good sign.

We'd been laughing not five minutes ago and now something was different.

"Nothing." She shrugged. "I had fun tonight. More than I thought I would."

"Me too. Though I had no doubts how much I'd have."

Her quiet laugh was barely audible in the breeze. "But I'm still confused."

"About?"

"What is this, Miller? It's so weird." She shook her head as if she weren't sure what to say or how to say it. "We weren't friends in high school. You were... not the nicest person, but you've been nothing but nice to me since you walked into the store and I'm over here waiting for the other shoe to drop. For the camera to pop out telling me it's all a joke."

"Hey." I yanked her arm to get her to stop. "It's not a joke." We were standing close to one another, her chest almost brushing my stomach and her full lips had one hundred percent of my attention.

Out here in the dim light, with the water beside us, would've been an excellent place for a first kiss. But that wasn't why I was here and I wouldn't do it before I knew she wanted me to either way.

"It's not a joke," I told her again. "High school was a long time ago."

She snorted. "Not for me."

"I haven't been there in a long time and I wasn't part of any of the pranks. Am I an asshole for not stopping them? Yes. But it wasn't me."

"I know. I knew even then it wasn't you who wrote the stuff on the bathroom wall but I think you do and even if I asked you wouldn't tell me, right?" When I didn't answer, she rolled her eyes and began moving again. I followed because I already had no choice. Wherever she was going, so was I and I cursed the fact that the coven had sent me to her.

"So then what is this?" she asked again, this time much quieter.

I knew what she was asking, but I had to think about my answer, given that I couldn't admit what I wanted tonight to be. Since this was technically a job for the coven, it wasn't supposed to get personal.

Yet it had.

Finally, I decided to screw the coven rules. This was a job for them, yes. But nothing was saying it couldn't be both.

"A date," I told her before I'd decided myself. But that was what this was. It was a date. No way around that. We'd spent time together, laughed, and overall had a good time. But it was the feelings that I didn't want to admit to that made it a date by anyone's definition.

"A date." Hazel wasn't looking at me. She was watching out in front of us as we kept walking. We'd made it almost around the pond in these few minutes. It wasn't a huge pond, but the silence between us must've stretched out longer than I'd thought. It was all going by too quickly. In no time we were going to be back at the house and she was going to disappear inside.

"You want me to stop asking things like that, don't you?" Her voice brought me back to what we'd just been talking about.

"Asking what?"

"What this is. If you're messing with me. All of that."

I scratched the back of my head. No way was I going to lie about this. "I would prefer you not question it so much, but I understand why you are. You can ask a million times if you want to, but if I'm being honest, Hazel, I had the biggest crush on you in high school, so asking you out tonight didn't take much convincing."

"Convincing?"

"Of myself," I answered quickly. "I didn't have to talk myself into it or hype myself up."

"Wait." She stopped, suddenly causing me to almost trip on her. Then she spun around to face me, her red hair flying out around her before settling on her shoulders again. "You just said you had the biggest crush on me in high school."

"Yeah." I smiled. "Because I did."

Her mouth softened and her lips parted. She made a sound like she was trying to say something, but nothing was coming out. Then she let out a loud groan and backed away from me.

"I can't believe you, Miller." She was stomping away from me and it took me a second to realize that I needed to get moving before she got around to the front of her house and was lost to me.

But where this anger was coming from, I didn't know.

"What'd I say?" I called out after her. "I was being honest."

She snagged her purse off the table she'd set it on when we'd come back here but kept her death march going.

"I just can't believe you, Miller. All of that garbage I dealt with and you're telling me that you liked me the entire time?"

"I was a fucking teenage boy. We're not known for our wise decision-making."

She snorted. "That much, I know. But you could've told me then. Or hell, *talked* to me so I didn't think you hated me."

"Did you care if I hated you?" None of it had

seemed to bother her much back then, so I couldn't be sure.

She suddenly turned to face me, causing me to come to a sharp stop.

"*Did I care*?" she yelled into the night air. "Of course I cared! If you knew how much I thought about you then, it would be embarrassing to me. I thought about you all the time. About how different things would be if I weren't so repulsive to you." Hazel threw her hands up and then was walking toward the front door again.

"Repulsive? Jesus Christ," I muttered as I scurried to follow her. She was almost on the steps when I grabbed her wrist. "You weren't at all," I told her. "Trust me... if our thoughts from then were on the table now, *I'd* be the one embarrassed."

"What's that supposed to mean?" She didn't try to get away from me.

I raised an eyebrow. "Think about it, Hazel. I was a sixteen-year-old guy."

Her cheeks turned a beautiful pink color that I instantly wanted to see again and again. "Oh my god."

She slapped a hand over her face as if what I'd said embarrassed her when in reality, the only person who should have felt anything near that was me. Somehow, I wasn't, though. Her knowing about back then... Turned out, that was what I wanted all along.

"This is ridiculous," she finally told me. "All of this wasted time..."

I moved in, grabbing her hips with each hand, then pulled her toward me. "How about we just not waste any more?" Mostly because we didn't have it to waste, but she didn't know that yet.

Everything I was telling Hazel was one hundred percent true, but I couldn't forget why I'd actually been sent to her. I had a job to do, but if in the end, I got that done and got the woman of my fucking dreams, I'd be ecstatic.

"Can we just act like none of that ever happened?" I asked her, knowing this was a big ask. She'd taken all of that shit really personally and I'd spend however much time necessary to make it all better.

"Yeah. Fine. We'll do that." She nodded as if agreeing with herself. "But I can't guarantee that if I see Oliver, I won't kick him in the nuts."

My chuckle was stark against the quiet night. "I won't even try to stop you."

"Good." She folded her arms just under her breasts. It took all of my willpower not to let my gaze falter from hers. "Wouldn't want you to get caught in the sweeping motion."

Yeah. Me, either.

"OK." She sighed heavily. "I'm going to go in and try to start processing all of this. Maybe eat a pint of ice cream." I would've offered to get her dessert but was pretty sure this was emotional comfort eating. "Good night, Miller."

"Good night."

Watching Hazel turn away from me and walk to her front door was hard when I wanted to sweep her up into my arms and kiss the hell out of her.

That would have to wait. I wasn't so sure it would've been a welcome move quite yet. Didn't matter how much I wanted it. I needed *her* to want it.

"Hey, Miller."

I turned at the sound of my name and Hazel was so much closer than she'd been before. She was moving quickly too.

Hazel didn't stop until she got up on her toes, leaned her head up, put her hands on either side of my face, and kissed me quickly. I didn't even have time to respond.

I reached out to pull her in closer so I could really kiss her, but she slipped right out of reach and walked backward toward the door.

"Hey, come back here."

She giggled. "Night, Miller."

I shook my head. "That's not fair."

She wiggled her fingers and then disappeared behind her front door.

Damn. That had barely been a kiss, but I was half hard from it. Like every teenage fantasy was coming true and I couldn't fucking wait.

7

MILLER

I COULD STILL TASTE HER ON MY LIPS FOR A LONG TIME after that kiss.

I even sent her a text saying as much.

The coven might've sent me to her, but at this point... I didn't care. This part was for me because I wasn't about to let Hazel slip through my fingers for a second time.

To be sure that I didn't rush her, I didn't see Hazel again that week. The calls and text messages weren't enough. The pics on Snapchat helped a little because at least then I could see her.

My alone time, I spent thinking about how I was going to tell Hazel she was a witch without freaking her the fuck out and I didn't talk to anyone about it. First of all, I should've been able to handle any job the coven threw my way and I wouldn't be the one to fail at it. Secondly, a big part of me wanted to keep Hazel all to myself.

If I talked to Luken and Oliver about all this, they'd offer to help, and eventually, I might've needed it, but right now... Right now, Hazel was all mine. They knew what the council had sent me on but had been good about not making it a bit deal. Yet.

Technically, I should've kept my hands off Hazel and my dick in my pants. I wasn't supposed to use any influence I might have over her to sway her choice. The council said that it had to be her choice, but damn. That rule was going to be difficult to follow.

In no world was I going to let Hazel choose the shadow coven over ours. Then she'd be lost to me forever.

"I thought you were working." Hazel's tired voice came through the phone, making me feel so much closer to her than I was.

"I am. I was." I sighed. "Listen, the festival is this weekend and I want you to go with me."

"Festival?" she asked, like she had no idea.

"Are you serious right now?" I snorted. "Hazel, everyone knows about the Summer Day's festival this weekend. Vendors. Activities. The picnic and movie in the park." *A perfect place to find out you're a witch.* I didn't add that last part or that I planned to put a protection spell on her after I told her.

Still had to make that, though.

"Oh, right. Yes. Sure I'll go with you. Want me to pack a picnic lunch?"

I scoffed. "Please. I invited you. I'll pack our picnic."

"If you bring a basket with only Cheetos and beef jerky, I'm going to leave."

I chuckled into the phone. "There goes my plans."

"Miller!"

"Take it down a notch. I know how to pack a picnic basket."

"I'm trusting you," she told me. "I tend to get hangry if I don't eat."

"Noted. I'll bring snacks for after, too."

Hazel snickered into the phone. "I always have an extra snack in my purse."

Beautiful, sweet, funny, and carries snacks at all times? I might have to marry this woman.

Fuck. I couldn't believe I'd even thought that. Though is shouldn't have surprised me.

The entire reason that I didn't do relationships

and said I didn't believe in true love was because it was never going to be Hazel. I couldn't have her so I didn't want anyone else.

On Saturday afternoon, Hazel came out of her house before I could get to the door.

She was wearing a pink strapless dress that hugged her in all the right spots but flared away from her at the hips. Her flat sandals meant she was still a lot shorter than me.

Up until now, I'd mostly dated taller than average women and was beginning to think it was because I didn't want them to remind me of her.

That was so fucked-up.

Her red hair was down and kind of wavy. I could imagine pulling those strands through my fingers.

"Hey." Her green eyes sparkled in the sunlight.

"You look..." I blew out a breath to show my appreciation. "Beautiful."

She rolled her eyes and shook her head. "This is just a sundress and it's super-hot today."

I shrugged. "You look fantastic." Hazel tried to keep from smiling so that I wouldn't see it, but I saw. With her, I always saw because of how fucking closely I watched her.

Once we were in the car and I was pulling out of

her driveway, I told her, "I packed us a lunch that I hope you'll like."

"I'm really not a picky eater."

"Still. Lots of water because it's pretty hot out, but it should be a good day."

"Sounds good to me." She settled back into the seat like it was the most comfortable thing in the world. "You know, if you would've had the courage to talk to me in high school, we could've saved some time."

"It wasn't that easy."

She snorted like she didn't believe me. "Of course it was but you didn't pay any attention to me back then."

"Hazel." I glanced over at her and held her gaze for as long as I dared before needing to watch the road again. "I always knew what you were wearing. Every single day. I knew your class schedule and who your friends were. I even know who wanted to ask you out. I paid a lot of attention."

"Gotcha there. Not a single person asked me on a date until after you graduated, so you couldn't have—"

I raised an eyebrow but kept my focus on the road, a smile playing at the corners of my mouth.

She still didn't know that I'd kept other guys

away from her for years. This might not have been the right thing to tell her, but it was all true.

"Did you..." She sighed. "Did you have something to do with that?"

"Maybe."

That was all she was going to get for now. The truth was that Luken and Oliver helped me keep guys away from her because not a fucking one of us was good enough.

"You know I haven't come to one of these since you graduated." We'd just gotten out of the car when she told me this.

"You serious? Don't you come every year?"

She shook her head as I came up beside her with the basket in my hand. "I came with my parents when I was a kid because I didn't have a choice, but once I started high school, I came only because I was hoping that you'd notice me." I folded her hand into mine and began walking toward the shaded area where I'd told the guys we'd find a spot. "Then when I realized you *had* noticed me and not in a good way, I still wanted to do this with friends, but we'd avoid you as best we could."

I'd seen her here every time, as if I'd been wired to locate her whenever she'd been around. "I noticed you, but I can't say it was in a good way."

"I know."

"No." I pulled her to a stop, keeping her hand in mine. "You don't. You say I didn't notice you in a good way, but it wasn't what you're thinking." I took a step closer to her and leaned down to whisper in her ear. "The thoughts in my head back then were very bad."

Hazel shivered as her back straightened, and her skin flushed. Not from the heat. When she swallowed hard, I knew she'd understood.

Laughter shook my chest as I tugged her hand to get her moving again.

Once we were under the biggest tree in the park with enough room around us for the others to join, I spread out the blanket I'd brought with me so that the two of us could sit. I still hadn't told her that Luken and Oliver were going to be there because I was worried she wouldn't have come if I had.

"I know I keep saying this, but it's really hard for me to believe it when you say things like that," she told me quietly as she watched the people around us.

Kids were running around near us, playing tag and laughing. There was a lot of laughter at these things. Not as much as say, the coven gatherings, but still a good time. This was one of the best parts of living in Echo Valley. How easygoing things were. The fact that most of the town still knew nothing about us witches surprised me, but it made things a lot easier.

"And that's my fault." I'd take full responsibility for that for the rest of my life if I had to. "But I'll prove it to you."

A smile crept over her face at the same time a large mass dropped down entirely too close to me.

Fucking Oliver.

"Found you," he said as he waved his hand next to him, indicating that he'd left enough space for Luken.

Fuck. He'd left enough space for Luken and at least three other people. He didn't need to be that close to me.

With the three of us, if Hazel didn't feel the power before I told her about being a witch, I'd be surprised.

"Great," I deadpanned.

"Hey, Hazel," he said, his eyes dancing with humor. I'd already warned him not to mess with her. He'd scare her off and make my life harder in all areas.

Hazel's jaw hardened. "Hello, Oliver."

"Shit. She definitely remembers me in high school."

"Don't we all?" I asked.

"So you invited them too?" she asked then sighed. "This is surreal."

"Oh." Oliver's eyes widened. "So you already told her—"

I cut him off. "No."

"Told me what?" Those big, green eyes slid away from Oliver and settled on me.

"Nothing. I'll tell you later."

Her jaw tightened again and she sat up straighter. *Great.* Now she thought I was hiding something from her, which of course I was. But not for much longer.

Oliver popped open his basket at the same time Luken joined us and did the same. Hazel was a bit warmer with Luken, as he hadn't been as mean as Oliver.

"So, is anyone going to explain why you were such jerks to me yet are acting like everything is perfectly fine now?" *Damn.* Hazel had called out the elephant in the park. "You guys were jerks back then."

"Yes," I said because there was no point in

denying it, but she already knew why I'd acted the way I had.

Oliver held up his hand. "I was the biggest, but it wasn't totally my fault."

Hazel cocked her red head to the side. "How's that?"

"Well..." He adjusted himself on the blanket. "I was an asshole because I was in love with a girl who hated me. Don't worry. It wasn't you."

She winced like she was disgusted. "I'd never think it was but that doesn't make sense," Hazel mumbled, like she was trying to figure out the hidden meaning.

Oliver rolled her eyes. "It's a long story. I'll tell you later. But..." He took a bite of his sandwich as he kept speaking. "I was an asshole to you, but it was because Miller was too much of a pussy to tell you how into you he was. It was crushing my best friend and I blamed you for it."

He spoke the truth and it didn't bother me a bit. Maybe hearing it from someone else, Hazel would believe me about how I'd felt about her back then. Those bright-green eyes jumped to me. I gave her a little nod as her tongue shot out and wet her lips.

Then she shook her head. "None of that makes any sense."

"It will," I told her. "Once you have the whole story and that time isn't now."

I needed to tell Hazel that she was a witch before we could get into most of that because explaining things would include talk of magic. Even though I hadn't known she was a witch then, it would be part of it.

After we finished eating, I gave Luken the nod that told him I needed some time alone with Hazel. I wasn't going to do it right there with so many people from town around. Seeing magic for the first time could freak a person out.

"Let's go for a walk," I told her quietly. She gave me a quick nod and then hopped to her feet.

As we walked away from my friends, I jammed my fists into my pockets to keep from touching her as we spoke. If I would've felt her smooth skin under my fingers, I didn't think we'd get to the conversation.

"Does this mean you're going to tell me what you're hiding?" she asked once we were away from the others.

I turned us down the walking path that would take us a little farther away from the festivities.

"Oliver explained it. He was telling the truth. I had it bad for you back then but was too much of a pussy to do anything about it." I swallowed hard. "There *is* something I want to tell you, though." My stomach tightened, hoping that she wouldn't freak out and never want to speak to me again or think I was absolutely out of my mind.

"Shoot." Hazel spoke like she didn't have a care in the world and I hoped it remained that way.

"There's no easy way to tell you this."

"That you're hopelessly in love with me?" A smile played on her lips and the corners of her eyes crinkled with humor.

"That's not far off," I told her honestly. There was no point in hiding it. I'd already told her how I felt. Just hadn't gone overboard with how I still felt. "But no. That's not what I wanted to tell you."

She came to a stop and turned to me. "OK. Tell me."

I took a deep breath and pulled my hands out of my pockets. I trailed my thumb down her cheek then snapped my hand away. Yeah, feeling her silky soft skin against mine had been a mistake. It threw me off.

"You're a witch, Hazel. I am too."

She shrugged, as if this weren't new information, then began walking again. "So the reason I ran out of my house today without letting you come to the door was that my parents were home. I don't think I've told you just how much I don't get along with them. I mean, besides them wanting me to go to their fundraisers. You'll be happy to know that I haven't caved, nor will I."

My mouth hung open slightly as I tried to make sense of this woman. I'd just told her she was a witch and she was talking about her parents.

"Hazel." I grabbed her upper arm and brought her to a stop. "Did you hear me?"

"Yeah. You said I was a witch. I heard you."

"And that's all you have to say?"

"I know you're messing with me, Miller. I don't know why, but how else should I respond?"

I wasn't sure what came over me as I slid my hands up her arms until I could cup her face. I leaned in and for the first time—well, the second, but the first didn't count because it was too quick and I wasn't ready for it—my lips pressed against hers.

Hazel moved in closer to me, her body pressing against mine. I'd always known that one taste of her wouldn't be enough. I ran my tongue across her lips, which made her open for me.

After that, I was lost in all things Hazel.

8

—————

HAZEL

IF THERE WAS ONE THING I KNEW ABOUT MILLER, IT was that he could kiss. Like, *really* kiss. Like, kiss a girl so that she forgot her name. I'd heard about it enough in high school because those girls hadn't been too shy to tell everyone what they'd been up to.

The kiss I'd given him when he dropped me at my house wasn't anything like this. It was scary in a different way because I'd never done that before. I'd never given a guy a hurried peck when we'd never kissed before.

I'd never experienced it myself until now. But even if those girls hadn't been chatty about it, I would've seen it in the way he carried himself. The cocky tilt to his head. Some guys had the cockiness and couldn't back it up, but given the things I'd heard about him back then, I knew that wasn't the case here.

As his mouth worked against mine and his hands slid up my back, I couldn't stop my mind from racing everywhere. Taking in all the sensations at once and pushing myself closer to him.

But most of all, I kept hearing the words he'd said right before he'd kissed me.

"You're a witch, Hazel. I am too."

As my fingers pushed into his hair, those words haunted me.

They couldn't be true, but what game was he playing? One that I was falling for it since I'd let him kiss me. And do that little move with his tongue that just now almost knocked my knees out from under me.

Then it occurred to me that there was something different about this town. As the words he'd said ran on repeat, I thought back to all of the weird things that I'd witnessed. Little things.

Like my blanket ending up on the floor this morning or my phone magically appearing in my pocket. Or the pencil that had flown across the room for no reason in high school. And I'd swear to this day that the book Luken had been looking at had the pages flipping rapidly without him touching it in health class my sophomore year.

I'd chalked it up to reading too many paranormal romance books.

But the pages had stopped as soon as he'd noticed I'd been watching.

I pulled away from Miller to catch my breath.

Could he have been telling me the truth? Was witchcraft real and he was one to wield it? Now I *knew* I wasn't a witch, but what about everything else?

"You OK?" he asked while trying to pull me by the hip. My feet stumbled on the grass, but I went.

Being close to Miller felt good. It felt right. While at the same time, everything felt wrong.

"Prove it," I told him as I pulled away again, my voice breathless even to my own ears. His lips were still slightly open and wet from what we'd just experienced. But my heart was racing, like it was trying to escape.

"What?"

"Prove it?"

"Prove what?" He reached out with his other hand to grab me by the hip. With both hands, he pulled me toward him without an issue.

I sighed. "You can't have forgotten what you just told me. Why are you confused about this?"

One corner of his mouth ticked up. "Your kiss made me forget everything else."

I groaned and rolled my eyes. He was smooth. I'd give him that.

"Come on." I slapped his shoulder lightly. "If you want me to believe you, you have to prove it, but, Miller..." I looked up at him through my lashes, almost shyly, though it was more that I feared this was an elaborate joke he was playing. "Please don't be messing with me. I don't..." I took a deep breath. Being with him in any way was scary for me, given what I'd believed to be our previous adversarial relationship, but now that he'd kissed me and shown me what I'd been missing... it'd be crushing to know he wasn't serious. "I don't think I could handle it."

As he stepped in even closer, his erection brushed against my stomach, sending a thrill of excitement through me. One that I was going to ignore.

"Hazel, I'm not messing you. I wouldn't."

Nodding, I bit my bottom lip and calmed myself. "Then prove it."

"Let's go." He folded my hand into his and began walking away so quickly that I had to take twice as many steps to keep up. "Not here, though, because there are too many nonwitches around."

Nonwitches? He was committed to this. "Makes sense. You're not taking me to some secluded area so that you can do away with me, are you?"

His deep chuckle made my body warm. "No, but if I were, would I tell you?"

"Yes," I said automatically. "Because you're only going to be honest with me from now on, right?"

"Right."

We were back to the guys quickly and I began to wonder if they all knew what he'd told me. Were they witches too?

I'd never wanted to be special in this way. Never wanted to be the chosen one or have supernatural powers.

I'd always wanted to blend into the crowd and even though Miller said he was a witch, too, that still meant we were different from regular people.

"Hazel and I are leaving." He'd waited until we were close to them before he spoke. "She wants me to prove it to her."

My head spun so that I could look up at him. They did know. Was I the only one who didn't? Or was this an elaborate prank.

I had to believe that as grown men, they'd be

beyond the high school shit they used to do and Miller had sounded so serious. Yet, still, I couldn't fully believe him either.

"That sounds fun." Oliver snorted.

"Could one of you take my basket and stuff with you?" he asked.

"Yeah, we got it," Luken said first.

Miller's eyes locked on mine and for the first time, I considered that he wasn't messing with me. I should say for the first time, I *seriously* considered that he wasn't messing with me.

Without further conversation, Miller was dragging me away from the guys.

"So they know that you're a..." I let my voice trail off because the idea of saying that he was a witch still hit me as absurd.

"That I'm a witch?" he whispered. "Yeah. They know because they are too. It's a whole thing."

"You're like..." I started. We stopped at his car and stared at each other over the hood. "A community within the community?"

"Yeah. Pretty much." He climbed into the car, so I did too.

If he was going to show me something amazing, I wanted to see it, yet part of my brain still rejected the idea of witches and magic. There was a tiny light in the deep recesses of my mind growing bigger, making me think that I'd already known this.

"It must be nice to have an extended family like that." I'd never had a regular family or at least not a loving, accepting one. "My parents aren't bad people." I had to pause to think about whether that was true or not. "Well, I don't think they are, but they aren't great parents."

His hand tightened on the steering wheel as he sped out onto the road. "Were they..."

"Abusive?" I finished for him. It was the likely conclusion after what I'd said. "No. Not physically. I think their mental gymnastics could be seen as... harmful, but I figured out how to protect against that when I was a kid."

"'Harmful'?"

"Yeah, I can't imagine the constant heavy guilt and pressure is good for a person."

As I watched Miller closely, I noticed every time his hand fisted against the steering wheel, every time the muscle in his jaw tightened. He wasn't enjoying this conversation at all.

"What?" I asked him.

"I hate that they do that to you. Pressure you at all, but my guess is the pressure has something to do with you being a witch. Or with magic."

I shot forward and turned toward him. "My *parents* aren't witches." As if I would've known either way.

"Yes, they are. You are, so they'd have to be. Or one of them has to be. I suppose that could work."

"You're insane. If my parents had magical powers or whatever, trust me, they would've used them to get me to do what they want."

He began shaking his head before I finished my sentence. "That's not how it works. At least not if those 'fundraisers' are what I think they are."

"What?"

He ran a hand through his hair. "Can I explain all of that later?"

What choice did I have? If any of this was true, he had the information I wanted and I couldn't force him to tell me everything all at once.

"Can't anyone become a witch? You said if I am, they have to be, but couldn't it just... be studied? Like a class?"

"No." He shook his head and then turned down a dirt road. "Anyone can be Wiccan because that's different. That's more like a religion. To be one of us, you have to be born to at least one witch. If it's one parent, the magic isn't as strong and you have to work harder. Unless you happen to be descended from either the Michigan or Salem witches. Those two lines are the most powerful, so just having one parent from those would make you incredibly powerful."

"Why is that?" I asked as we both stepped out of his car at the end of the dirt road. There was a small area, almost an alcove, surrounded by trees. I wondered why this road was here at all and how he knew about it, but those were questions for a different time. "Why would a descendant of one of those be so powerful?"

"Slow down." He came to a stop right in front of me. Close enough that my breasts almost brushed against his... well, I'd like to say chest, but I wasn't tall enough. More like his upper-ish abdomen.

Miller ran his hand through his hair and blew out a breath. "Those lines are super old and incredibly powerful. Their magic doesn't need a boost from a second witch because it's kind of..." He scratched at his jaw, like he was thinking of the right words. "Original magic. That's not exactly right, but it's the best description I can think of."

"What do you mean, 'original magic'?"

"The origin of our magic comes through the witches from Salem and the witch trials, and the Mackinac Island trials. Those two cities were the first lines of witches settled. In Salem, they hung witches and some innocents. On the island, they had drowning pools. Many witches sacrificed themselves rather than out what we are, knowing outing us would've been worse."

My eyes widened. It wasn't every day that someone told you that one of the biggest scams perpetrated on a group of people was real. "They were really witches?"

"Some of them were, but some of them weren't. Most of the witch families were able to remain undiscovered, mostly due to the sacrifices of those who gave their lives."

"I have so many questions," I whispered.

"They can wait." As I was about to protest, he held up a hand. "I'll answer all of your questions, but right now, you wanted me to prove it, so let me prove it."

I bit down on my bottom lip and nodded.

"Now," he began, "we are elemental witches, which means we call on the elements. There are spells and potions that you don't directly need to call on any of the elements to make work, but for the magic that you alone summon, you need at least one." He moved away from me several steps while I remained cemented to my spot. "The easiest is earth because we use it to ground ourselves for everything else. Some of us can call them all at once without even trying, but that's rarer. Some of us, like me, can call all of them because I've had decades of training."

Miller took a deep breath and held out his arms. I didn't know what I was watching for, but it was kind of beautiful. His head fell back and the next thing I knew, this barren little spot at the end of a dirt road, surrounded by trees, was flooded with beautiful white flowers.

"What in the...?"

Miller chuckled and then waved his hand, which caused poison ivy to curl around the flowers.

I liked it better the other way.

"You..." I sputtered, trying to get my thoughts together.

"Do you believe me now?"

"You made those flowers grow?" I asked with disbelief.

He nodded enthusiastically. "I thought this would be an easier, safer way to prove it to you."

"Safer?"

"I didn't want to do a spell that could go wrong. Mine don't tend to, but anything could happen and I don't want to hurt you on accident." He closed the distance between us and then reached out for me. "Believe me now?"

"I'm not sure I have a choice." I swallowed hard. I couldn't believe that all of this had been going on in my town my entire life and I'd never known anything about it. "I'm allergic to poison ivy." He'd began to move like he'd wanted to take me into the flowers.

Miller chuckled then waved his hand and the ivy disappeared, allowing me to enter the field of flowers with him.

"I feel... overwhelmed right now," I told him honestly. "I'm not sure what to make of this and you're trying to tell me that I can do these things?"

He nodded. "With training. It's easier when we start as kids like I did and like Oliver did, but Luken didn't know until he was fifteen. He's a quick learner."

"What about me? How would I learn all of this?"

A sheepish grin appeared on his face. "I'll teach you if you want me to. Oliver and Luken will help."

My mood darkened when he mentioned those two, but that was something I'd have to deal with. I'd thought this was something Miller intended to do. I had no problem spending any time with Luken and I'd get past anything Oliver did when we were kids but I wanted the alone time with Miller.

"*Want* to?" I laughed loudly. "You're telling me that I can do magic and just proved that magic exists. I don't think there's a question of wanting to. When can we start?"

I thought he was going to kiss me again, but my phone beeped from the pocket in my dress and after I glanced at it, I groaned.

"My parents have made it clear that they need to meet me at the bookstore. Right now, apparently. They're in town and thought I was working." I shook my head and looked back up at him. "I'm sorry. I have to go."

His jaw tightened as he took my hand. "I asked you before not to go to your parents' functions..."

"And I haven't."

We stopped next to the passenger-side door of his car. "I don't want to freak you out," he said, "but you need to be careful. Of everyone."

"What do you mean?" There was a tightening in my stomach... Dread.

Miller quickly wet his lips. "It's been my experience that, except for Luken, the parents who keep magic from their kids, at least in our town, do so for some not-so-great reasons."

"Like what?"

"Well, there's a shadow coven that has been trying for decades to siphon witches away from our coven. I'm told they'll use any means necessary, but to go to that coven, it has to be a choice. You have to make that choice."

"I won't make it, then."

He shook his head. "It's not as simple as that. They can trick you, Hazel. Make you think it's a good thing, but the one thing they can't do is lie. I mean they can in the beginning, but when you make your oath, you have to know what it's to." He took a quick breath. "It's complicated, but if you choose to be a witch of light magic and join our coven, you'll know that's what you're doing. They have to do it too, but I've been told they'll do things to make it impossible for you to choose anything else."

"But you just said they can't force me."

"They can't." He let out a sigh of frustration. "But say the entire rest of your family whom you adore chooses the shadow coven. You might not feel like there's any other option for you."

"Oh. No worries about that. They can have my parents." Though the idea of my parents being witches still hadn't fully materialized as truth. They were assholes, sure. Witches? That wasn't so clear.

But if they were and they'd kept this from me, then it gave me a whole new reason not to trust them.

"Listen." He came close, taking up all of my personal space. "I don't know what happened years ago, but it was bad and people were hurt. I don't want that to happen to you."

I swallowed hard before saying the words I knew to be true. "You won't let it."

"I won't." He said it like a vow or a promise that I knew he'd make sure he kept until his last breath.

"All of this is... a lot," I told him.

"I know." He brushed a stray piece of hair away from my face. His touch was gentle, causing me to break out in goosebumps. "But since your parents are witches and they're not part of our coven, that means they must belong to another. I don't know for sure if it's the dark one we've been trying to keep away or not, but... I worry about you."

His words melted me. "I promise, Miller. I won't go to any of their things. I've been fending them off my entire life, so it'll be easy. But the bookstore isn't a dark anything and I have to go meet them."

"Why?"

"I've learned to play the game," I told him honestly. "I know which things I can stand my ground on and which I can't. They're paying for my life right now and until I graduate or figure out another way, I have to play their game to some extent."

"Or you could move in with me. I have a job and can pay for your life."

The intensity in his eyes told me that he was absolutely serious. He'd take me in, but I also knew that I couldn't let him do that anyway.

"Miller, you can't pay for my tuition. Neither can I and I worry that if we move this thing too fast, it's going to blow up in our faces." Though his offer had me rethinking everything all of a sudden. I had a job, part-time, and began to wonder what full-time would look like.

"Those in the coven take care of each other."

I slid my hand up the side of his face and let my fingers settle into his hair before pulling him closer. "Let me see what they want and I'll think about everything. You've put me on alert and I won't let them trick me into anything. This little field will be our place when I need to get away."

Miller's hands rested on the car behind me, his body pushing into mine like my very own Miller cage. "Anything, Hazel... you need anything or they trying anything... you call me."

My skin tingled at both his offer and his warning because there was no doubt that his words were both.

"I will."

His lips crashed into mine and this was more than hormones taking over for either of us. This wasn't his need to kiss me. This was his need for me to know that I was his. The best part was that I wanted to be.

9

———

MILLER

HAZEL WAS STILL DAZED WHEN I DROPPED HER AT home.

I liked to think that it was my kissing, but more likely, it was the fact that I'd shown her that magic was real to prove that she was a witch.

Her having to leave made it a little worse. I'd thought when I showed her a little something about magic, we'd have all night to talk it through and maybe see what she could do naturally, if anything at all. But no. She wanted to go home to get her car so that she could go meet up with her parents.

Why were her parents meeting her at the book-store? Why not at home?

Nothing about this felt right and all of my witchy

senses were on high alert. Getting her a protection charm was now my top priority.

I headed back to the park because Oliver and Luken would've still been there. It was easy to find them looking at the classic cars that came from all over for this festival.

Hazel going to the bookstore alone had me on edge. It was like my skin was too small for my body and it was a reminder that I didn't need as to why I'd never wanted to get into a relationship in the first place. But I couldn't push this too hard. I'd seen it happen before and if I pushed her the way her parents did, I'd probably lose her too.

My dad had always been extremely protective of my mom. Hated it if my mom even went to the store without him. He didn't stand in her way, but I always knew when Mom was gone based on Dad's behavior.

Now I kind of understood it.

She was out there without anyone to look out for her.

Except me, when I was with her. Hazel only had me as far as I could tell.

"Where's Hazel?" Oliver asked as I approached them.

"She had to meet her parents."

Luken raised an eyebrow. "Did you tell her—"

"Of course I did. She's aware, even if she doesn't understand."

"What's that mean?" Oliver asked.

I let out a sigh as I stepped closer to the two of them so the entire town wouldn't be privy to coven business. "It means that I told her she's a witch. Showed her that I am, but that doesn't mean it's sunk in completely. It's going to take time."

"I'm not sure how much time we have." Luken glanced around us, like he wanted to make sure no one had heard him.

"What's that mean?"

"Nothing." He waved me off. "We'll talk about it later."

I furrowed my brows. That wasn't like him. Usually, when he had something to say, he'd say it, but I let it go anyway. If he wasn't talking, there was a reason.

"OK," I told them. "Anyway. She knows."

"Good. You think her parents are part of the shadow coven?" Oliver asked. I nodded and he threw his hands in the air in frustration. "What's the shadow coven giving them that ours can't? It's got to be something big, right? For them to try to get their own kids into their dark shit?"

I shrugged. That was the million-dollar question, now wasn't it?

"Don't parents normally want their kids to follow them?" I asked. Didn't seem odd to me that they'd want her in the same coven, want her powers there, but what I didn't get is why they would've chosen the shadow coven in the first place.

The shadow coven had come out of the darkness years ago. The council, which had been headed by Serena Goode back then, had done what they could to fight against them. Even Serena couldn't stop members of our coven from defecting and she'd been one of the most powerful witches to exist. Pure magic had run through that woman's veins and they'd done their best.

Once she'd left, things had gotten harder, but I didn't know the details. For a coven that wanted to protect against dark magic, the council were awfully secretive about the things that had happened in the past.

"How'd she take it?" Luken asked as moved on to another car. We were looking but not paying attention.

"Better than I probably would've."

"Or maybe it hasn't hit her yet," Oliver offered.

"Maybe." That was what I'd been thinking too.

Hazel hadn't had time to process much. I'd told her a lot in a short amount of time. "It's going to take time."

"Didn't look like it to me," Oliver said under his breath, but he'd clearly intended for me to hear him.

I stopped in front of a cherry-red Mustang. "What do you mean?"

"You came back holding her hand. I assume some things happened where we couldn't see you. Doesn't look like it's going to take much time to me."

"Fuck off."

Oliver chuckled. I should've expected this, given the years I'd dodged any chance at a relationship. He wasn't talking about the witch stuff at all.

"It's OK to admit you like this assignment," Luken added.

I shook my head.

"You know that's not what this is," I told him, folding my arms over my chest. I'd known Oliver my whole life. Both of them had witnessed my broody, tortured teen years when I'd been pining for Hazel. "This wouldn't be me falling in love on an assignment and you know it."

"That's true." Oliver tried not to smile. "Miller's had a hard-on for Hazel since she got to the high school."

He snapped his fingers loudly. "Oh, that's right." The sound of Luken's voice made me want to gut-punch him. He spoke like he didn't know this the whole time and was just realizing it now when in reality, we all knew I'd had a thing for Hazel then and the two assholes were harassing me. We didn't need to rehash it and he sure as shit remembered too. This play-acting like he'd forgotten got under my skin. "I never did understand why you didn't just talk to her then."

"Can we not discuss this right now?" I asked with a sigh.

"Why not?"

"Maybe we should talk about the fact that Oliver owes Hazel a better apology?"

His brows furrowed. "What'd I do? I explained why."

Luken snickered before answering. "You were a pretty gigantic dick to her back then."

"A super dick," I added.

Oliver groaned. "That was only because—"

"Doesn't matter." I cut him off. "I already apologized to her and the next time you see her, you should too. A better one than you did at the picnic."

"I don't have a problem doing it," he began. "But

I don't think it's my fault. You wanted to keep her away. I helped do that."

I nodded because I couldn't argue with him there. "Still. I think it'll make her feel more comfortable."

He held his hands up in defeat. "Like I said, I don't have a problem apologizing. I just wanted it clear that I wasn't a dick to her because I wanted to be. I was being a good friend to you. You might not have wanted to tell us why you were keeping her away." I tried to protest. "No really. You never fully explained it, but it's not like we know. I knew."

"So did I," Luken added.

"But I will be sure to tell her how sorry I am the next time I see her."

"That's all I'm asking."

"So Danna told me something interesting," Luken said as we got to the end of the cars.

Danna, the token young person on the council. It wasn't unusual for her to give us insider information, but it was unusual for her to give it to Luken. Unless... *Oh, fuck.* They were hooking up again. That had to be it.

"We don't need to know the freaky stuff," I told him. Oliver snorted beside me.

"Fuck off." He gave me a light push and then

chuckled. "As part of the council, she's hearing a lot of things that've got her suspicions up."

"Suspicions of what?" Oliver asked. "What's she hearing?"

"She hasn't wanted to go into details just yet because she says it could all mean nothing."

"If she's mentioning it," I countered. "Then she thinks it's something."

He nodded. "I know. I thought maybe we could all talk. Like a group and then she'd let us help her figure out if it's something to worry about or not."

"That's a good idea," I told him.

"But," he continued, "from what she *has* said, I think it's about the council and the shadow coven. Or at least part of the council."

Uneasiness roiled my stomach. That would be a game changer and not in a good way. If any part of our council had anything to do with the shadow coven, it could be catastrophic for us all.

I swallowed hard before asking, "Does she mean that *our* council is actually the shadow coven? Or at least working with the shadow coven?"

He shook his head. "She didn't say that. But we should talk."

"Today?" I asked because I did have something else that I needed to get done.

"Later tonight. She said she could meet around ten. My place."

"Convenient," Oliver muttered under his breath, but we all heard it and I had to hold back a snort.

Danna and Luken weren't a love match, but they also couldn't seem to stay away from each other. No. That wasn't true. They stayed away from one another whenever Danna had a boyfriend. Luken wasn't about to stab another witch in the back. We were a small club that took care of each other.

Just seemed he took better care of Danna sometimes.

"That works for me," I told them. "I'm going to head to my parents to make Hazel a protection charm." I shook my head. "Something about her parents has me on edge and I've never met the fuckers."

"But you trust your gut," Oliver finished my thought.

I shrugged. "I have to, right? That's what we do."

"I'll come with you," Oliver offered. "Make sure you don't fuck it up."

"I'm not going to—never mind. Come on."

The two of them agreed to meet me at my parents' house. It wasn't quite dark yet, but the sun had started to set, which meant it was a perfect chance to get an amulet charged. And I didn't doubt that my parents had everything I was going to need.

Like the good witches they were, everything was kept in a room not easily accessible by nonwitches. As a matter of fact, the room was spelled so that any nonwitch who tried to open the door would find that they couldn't.

I didn't have a room like this set up yet because I lived in an apartment and with my parents right there, why bother?

Luken and Oliver both parked on the street while I pulled into the driveway and parked out back like I always did, but instead of going in through the kitchen, I joined them out front and went in through the front door.

"What are you boys doing here?" Mom asked as she hopped up off the couch where she'd been reading to come over and hug me while kissing my cheek. She did the same with Luken and Oliver. She'd known them so long that she said they were like her own.

Mom still looked so young. Partly because she had good genetics and partly because she was. She'd had me pretty young. Her strawberry-blonde hair didn't have a hint of gray yet, though Dad's did. He said it was because dark hair grayed faster, but I didn't know about that.

"I need to make a protection amulet," I told her once she was done greeting us.

Her face grew concerned. "What'd you do?"

I furrowed my brows. Mom was a small woman, but when she was worried about me or my friends, she could've taken down a full-grown dragon if she had to.

"Why do you think I did something?"

"Why else would you need an amulet for protection?"

The guys were snickering behind me. "It's like she knows you too well." Oliver clapped my shoulder as if he'd never gotten himself into trouble before.

Mom turned to him. "Do you think you're any better? I assume that whatever Miller has gotten into, you're part of it. Both of you."

Now *I* was the one smirking. He couldn't have thought my mother was going to let him off the hook.

"It's not for me," I told her. "Not for us. We haven't done anything."

She raised an eyebrow but didn't say anything, like she was still skeptical.

"It's for Hazel Riley. You remember Hazel, right?"

"Of course I do. What's happened?"

"Didn't Dad fill you in?" I asked, but she shook her head. So in the quickest way possible, I told her about my job for the coven and my suspicions about Hazel's parents since they were the reason I wanted to make the amulet.

Mom nodded slightly until I finished. "Right. Then make sure you do the spell right and if you need my help, I'm here." The three of us began to walk away until she said, "Miller, if she needs to leave her house, she can come here. She can stay in your old room for as long as she needs." I wanted to thank her and tell her that wouldn't be necessary, but the concern on my mother's face had deepened, causing lines that weren't normally there.

"Sorry, Mrs. Campbell," Oliver started and I knew I wasn't going to like what he had to say. "If she's staying somewhere, my guess is it wouldn't be in Miller's *old* room."

I clenched my jaw and grabbed my friend by the back of the neck to yank him from the room. But at least Mom had snickered and the tiny grin that had replaced the furrowed brow fit her better.

The three of us found what we needed in the potion room and then headed to the back yard. I probably should've left these dummies at the festival, though it would've ended by now. As a matter of fact, it had grown just dark enough for the fireworks display to start.

The three of us formed a circle in the back yard, where I placed the amethyst between us.

First, we needed to cleanse the necklace. Who knew what other spells it had absorbed in the past?

I lit the bundle of white sage and then blew on it until smoke was billowing slowly from it. Luken picked up the necklace making sure that the amethyst was hanging loosely so that I could hold the sage beneath it.

All of us were very serious because this wasn't something to mess with. There was no room for jokes when it came to witchcraft. Even Oliver had a serious look on his face with no sign of the playfulness that was usually his main personality trait.

Once it had burned enough to cleanse the amulet, I set the sage in the middle where the necklace had previously been. The smoke continued to rise.

Oliver looked up over his shoulder. "It's a waning moon."

"Perfect." Luken set the necklace over the sage.

The three of us relaxed our shoulders and took a

few deep breaths. This would work better if we were in a full ritual state of mind. Then I picked the necklace up and held it in my hand while Luken and Oliver each covered the top with one of theirs.

I could've done this alone, but they were right. Having the three of us should've made it stronger.

"Visualize," Oliver said as he closed his eyes. Luken and I did the same so that each of us could visualize the protection that we wanted the amulet to give Hazel. Protection from her parents and protection from the shadow coven.

It wouldn't take away her free will if she was to choose the shadow coven, but at least, for now, she'd have a level of protection when I couldn't be there.

We poured our energy into that stone and held it like that for fifteen minutes. I didn't time it, but it was at least that.

When we broke, Oliver blew out a breath. "I'm beat."

Because all of our energy had gone into charging the amulet.

"Where are you going to put it?" Luken asked.

I stood and waved for them to do the same.

"Mom had Dad build her a moon box years ago. That's where we put it because the mirrors inside ensure that no matter where the moon is, it will direct the moonbeams to the amulet." I walked them over to the side of the house to show them the box and put the amulet inside.

"That's smart," Oliver agreed.

"I'll have to remember that you have this," Luken told me. "In case I ever need it."

"You guys can use it whenever you want. You know we won't put another one in there if there's already one."

Once this thing was fully charged, I'd be able to breathe a little easier because something inside me told me that Hazel just wasn't safe.

And unless I wanted to quit my job to hover over her twenty-four hours a day, this was going to be the next best thing.

Don't think I wouldn't do it... quit my job. But me hovering would've been the quickest way to scare Hazel off and that was the last thing I wanted to do.

I wanted to protect her from whatever was coming.

10

———

HAZEL

Driving to the bookstore filled me with dread. Dread wasn't an unusual emotion for me to experience when dealing with my parents. Now... it was different. Not meeting at the bookstore because if my parents were in town when they needed something from me, that was where we'd meet up. Especially if they were going to be staying in town. It made no sense for any of us to drive home then come back.

Miller had told me that I was a witch. I still didn't know if I believed him or not, but he'd more than proven to me that *he* was. Assuming witches were real, but if they weren't, how in the hell could he have done that in the field while I'd been watching?

Somewhere along the way, I'd convinced myself to suspend disbelief and trust him.

I blamed the kiss. His molten-hot mouth on mine had taken all of my sense away. On the one hand, I didn't know Miller well. Only spending time together for a few days of the last couple of weeks, though we did text. But on the other, I'd known him since we'd been kids. The only issue was that he was a jerk back then. A jerk I fantasized but a jerk, nonetheless.

One thing was certain. I'd promised to be on my guard with my parents and I'd do that. I'd always done that, but now the weird vibe I'd gotten most of my life might have a reason behind it.

I parked behind the bookstore and much to my surprise, they were already there

In the dark.

Behind a closed bookstore where I worked.

Now I didn't want to get out of the car.

Taking a deep, calming breath, I jerked the handle rougher than I needed to. It might've not been the best idea to get out of the car to face them, but I lived with them and maybe if I continued to pretend to be completely in the dark about whatever they were doing, I'd be fine.

Besides, Miller had suspicions, not certainty. My parents might have been dark witches or they could just have been terrible parents.

Only time would tell.

I wanted to believe Miller because I didn't want to think he'd lie to me. Yet my brain was still having a hard time wrapping around the idea that I had witchcraft at my fingertips that I didn't know how to use or that my parents were witches, too.

"Why'd you want to meet me here?" I asked, standing as far from them as possible while still looking like I wanted to be there.

"We have someone for you to meet."

I furrowed my brows. I could've met this person at home. Unless... there was a reason he couldn't go to our house.

Wait. If witches were real, did that mean other supernatural creatures were too? Werewolves? Vampires? Little sprites that danced in the forest?

Discovering the truth behind that idea was something that would have to wait until later.

A tall man, maybe just shy of Miller's height, got out of another car that I'd noticed sitting there, though I hadn't seen anyone inside. He had lighter hair, but the sun was too far gone for me to get a good look at him.

But I got a good enough one for the hair on my arms to stand up.

"This is our friend's son, Kingston," my father told me as the man walked toward me.

I swallowed hard and prepared myself to run back to my car.

"He's twenty-four," my father continued. "Good upbringing. We think you two would be a good fit."

"Hi," was all Kingston eked out, given that my father was doing all of the talking.

"Hi," I said back without looking at him. For all I knew, Kingston was an innocent bystander to my parents' crazy. "What're you doing?" That question was directed at my father.

My mother was there, leaning against the car with her ankles crossed. When shit like this was going on, she tended to leave it to my father to do all the talking.

"Your mother and I saw you with the Campbell kid in the park today."

My spine straightened and all of my red alert alarms began blaring in my head. "I ran into a couple of people I went to high school with."

He pursed his lips and narrowed his eyes like he didn't believe me. I didn't need a clear view of my father to know that face. "I'm hoping that's all it was."

"It was."

"Well..." He shrugged. "Even so, your mother and I thought it was time to introduce you to someone appropriate and we were in town."

"'Appropriate'?" I echoed. He nodded, so I snorted. "Are you trying to get me laid, Dad?"

His face reddened immediately. I would've understood it if he weren't completely used to my sassy comebacks. I might've had to deal with my parents because of school and life, but I didn't tiptoe around my contempt.

"That's disgusting, Hazel," my mother snapped.

"Well, that's what this sounds like." I waved my hands around to indicate the entire scene. "You have me meet you in a dark parking lot at night to set me up with him." I pushed my thumb in Kingston's direction. "What else am I going to think?"

My father's jaw tightened. "We're trying to do what's best for the family, Hazel." He took several intimidating steps toward me so he could use his size and bulk to put fear in me.

It didn't work anymore.

"Eventually," he continued, "you're going to get with the program and do what's right too. It's only a matter of time."

I steeled every muscle in my body so that none

would betray me. While I never let my father know that his fear tactics worked, they sometimes did.

"I hope you have fun waiting," I told him then scurried back to my car before he had a chance to respond.

Once I was pulling away from them, my trembling hands made steering difficult. When there was enough distance between them and me, I pulled over to take a few deep breaths. Then I did something that I would never have been able to guess I would have just a few days ago.

I called Miller.

The call went to voicemail and I didn't want to leave a message. But hearing his voice, even for a second, had the calming effect that I desperately needed. It got me through so I could get back home. But first, I stopped at a store for some drinks and snacks because nothing short of a fire was going to get me out of my room tonight.

My parents weren't home when I arrived, which was a good thing. My father hated it when I walked away and I didn't want to hear about it. All I wanted were my comfortable pajama pants, a ponytail holder, and alone time. *Oh, let's not forget the lock on my door.* Though I thought he could've broken it down if he wanted to.

Tonight, I pulled a chair over in front of the door, just to make sure he didn't come in. My father had never done anything like that before, but he'd been pissed when I'd left him the parking lot, so I wasn't going to chance it.

Now that I was comfortable, I pulled my laptop over and began a deep dive.

Witches.

Supernatural creatures.

Spells.

It led me down some dark rabbit holes that I never wanted to revisit. But there was one site that may or may not have been real, though it seemed to be the most credible.

The site went into the Salem witch trials being a stain on the history of witches. Especially since many of the women who'd been killed had been innocent and had died protecting our secrets.

Our.

I guessed I was embracing the witch thing.

But the part I found most intriguing was the section on spells and how to cast them. Some needed ingredients, others didn't. I focused on the ones that didn't.

Simple ones.

Easy ones.

The spells for beginners who needed training wheels.

I breathed deeply. I focused. I tried to ground myself, whatever that meant. I did everything it said to do and... nothing happened.

"Well, that was anti-climactic," I murmured to my empty room.

What was I thinking? Like I'd suddenly be able to do spells.

I rolled my eyes and fell back against my pillow to stare at the ceiling.

My mind wandered from the idea of being a witch to Miller. The boy I'd loved in high school. And nobody could tell me it wasn't love just because we hadn't been together. Maybe it had been puppy love, I didn't know, but it had been real. My feelings for him had been real and him now being in my life had brought all of them back to the surface.

All I could think about was how he'd kissed me. How his tongue had brushed over mine. How my nipples had pebbled against the warm night air simply because he'd run his hands down my arms as we'd kissed. Without a bra. There was no way he hadn't noticed, either.

It made me wonder if I affected him that way. Though I *had* felt what I'd thought had been the start of an erection against my stomach when he'd pulled me close.

I clenched my thighs together at thoughts of what that erection might have looked like if I'd taken it out of his jeans. I'd wanted to. Right there in public, but that wasn't something I'd ever do. I wasn't an exhibitionist, but the braver side of me was.

I brushed my fingertips over the soft skin on my chest and continued down before gently running over one of my nipples. Was I really going to do this at a fantasy involving Miller Campbell?

Yeah. I think I was.

Continuing down the path, my eyes fluttered closed. It'd been so long since anyone else had touched me this way and while it wasn't totally foreign for me to touch myself, it wasn't a regular thing, either.

But Miller had me on edge. Thinking about him helped me forget about all things having to do with my parents.

I gently pushed my shirt up a bit before sliding my hand into my shorts and then through my own curls. I kept things pretty tidy down there, but not bare.

Teasing myself, I tickled over the sensitive skin

twice before deciding that I couldn't take the teasing. Instead, I landed exactly where I needed it.

I rubbed the sensitive nub gently while picturing all the things I'd like to do with Miller. The movie playing in my mind was definitely rated NC-17.

He kissed down my neck while thrusting his hand into my shorts, much like I was doing right now. He dropped to his knees and kissed down my stomach, then he peeled the shorts off my body and pushed my thighs apart.

It was too much. I was too eager. An orgasm rocked my body as I bit my lips closed before I even got to the good part of my fantasy. Instead of imagining how talented that tongue might've been, I was left trying to catch my breath with my legs spread on my bed.

As I came down from the high, one that I somehow knew would pale in comparison to what Miller could make happen, my phone rang.

I sat straight up and yanked my hand out of my pants as I grabbed it. In my little bubble, I had no idea if my parents were home or if this was them.

But I was pleasantly surprised to see it was Miller.

"Hey," I answered, hoping that my voice didn't sound like I'd just been doing what I'd been doing.

"Hey. You called. Sorry I didn't answer. I was working on something." The sound of his voice shot desire through my veins, even though I'd just had a release.

"I-It's no problem. You're allowed to be busy."

"Yeah, but I never want to miss your call. What's up?"

"Nothing," I said quickly. "I wasn't doing anything."

He chuckled on the other end of the phone. "I have to say you sound hella guilty about something."

I slapped a hand over my face as my skin began to burn. "I don't think so. I just meant that nothing was going on."

"Uh-huh." He didn't sound convinced. "We'll come back to that. Did you just want to talk earlier? I can come get you."

"No." I shook my head, even though he wouldn't be able to see it. "It was after I'd talked to my parents and they got under my skin. No big deal."

"What happened?"

I sighed. While I was still feeling warm and mushy inside, I really didn't want to talk about my parents. "Can I just tell you tomorrow? Or whenever I see you again? I don't really want to rehash it right now."

"Sure. Yeah. About that. You busy tomorrow?"

"Nope. Don't even work."

"It's going to be hot as hell, but I was thinking we could go out to the lake and start training."

The lake wasn't huge, but it was where people from town spent a lot of their summers. Which meant there'd be people around. "But it gets crowded there."

"Not where I'm thinking. I want us to go to the other side of the swim area. There's a cabin out there with a dock and no one else for a while. It'll be perfect. No one can get hurt."

My heart sputtered in my chest. "Hurt?" I asked.

"You're not going to hurt anyone, but when you're learning, spells can go wrong. This is where I started teaching Luken. Trust me."

I did trust him. "Yeah. Sure. What time do you want me there?"

"I'll pick you up. Does ten work for you? We could grab breakfast first. Unless you're an early eater."

I wasn't. Actually, I didn't like to eat when I first woke up, so that time worked for me. "Ten is good."

"Then it's a date." The briefest moment of silence passed before he went back to the one thing I didn't want him to know about. "So, what were you doing before I called to make you sound guilty?"

"Nothing. I don't feel guilty about anything."

"Hmm…" I could imagine him stroking his chin as he tried to come up with a scenario or word and right now, I was glad it was the only thing I imagined him stroking. "If not *guilty*, then caught. What'd I catch you doing?"

I groaned and threw myself on my bed then pulled the pillow over my head. "You're not going to let this go, are you?"

"What? You're muffled."

I sighed and moved the pillow. "You're not going to let this go, are you?"

"No. Especially if it's what I hope it is."

Did I want to know? Yes, yes I did. "What do you want me to have been doing?"

"I don't know if I should tell you," he whispered huskily. I kept my mouth shut and waited. "Fine. I will." It had taken exactly zero convincing. "I want you to tell me you were thinking dirty things about me. I want you to tell me that you were touching yourself while thinking those dirty thoughts. I really want to hear how you came all over your own fingers while touching yourself and thinking dirty thoughts about me."

I slapped a hand over my face because of how damn accurate he was right there and began to wonder if he could read minds. Not a question I was going to ask right now.

"Hazel?" he prodded.

"I... It's not..." I stammered—and I never stammered.

"Am I embarrassing you? I'm sorry. I don't get embarrassed, so I forget other people might." He took a breath and as he blew it out, it feathered against his phone. "How about this: If you *were* doing all of those things, you don't have to tell me, obviously, but you could also just stay silent for a second and I'd know."

I bit my lips together again to keep the donkey cackle from erupting from my chest.

"Fuck," he whispered because my silence was my admission.

"Miller..."

"That's insanely hot, Hazel."

"Why did you have to call right then?" I asked, hoping that the humor I intended came through. His loud laugh was evidence that it had.

"I'm fucking glad that I did."

I groaned, which was followed by him saying, "Make that noise again."

"Miller!"

"All right. All right." His laughter died down. "I'll see you in the morning."

I shook my head as I said goodnight and ended the call, not able to believe that I'd really just admitted to all of that, more or less.

Tomorrow was going to be awkward as hell, but I'd get through it. Anything if it meant he was going to teach me witch stuff so that I'd be better prepared for whatever my parents had planned.

11

MILLER

Thinking about Hazel touching herself while picturing me gave me the hardest erection of my life.

It also made it difficult to sleep. When I finally did nod off, I was tormented with dreams of her. Tormented in the best way. However, when I woke, I had to remind myself that getting inside her wasn't my only goal.

Protecting her had to take priority because the way I felt about her already meant that I wouldn't be able to handle something happening to her. And I was sure that her parents were up to something.

If her parents were part of the dark coven and the council knew, I assumed they'd tell me. But assuming hadn't worked out for me in the past. I sent Luken a text asking him to ask Danna. Sure, I could've reached out to her myself. Having him do it added a little bit of fun to this situation.

Even with my restless sleep, I was up, showered, and ready to go in time to pick Hazel up.

"Where are you off to?" Dad's voice brought me to a stop. I hadn't thought anyone was outside as I'd hurried to my car. He was inside the garage with a coffee cup in his hand.

"Picking up Hazel," I told him. There was no reason for me to hide what I was doing. "Taking her out to the lake to see if we can figure out what she can do."

"Training?"

I nodded. "But hey, I wanted to ask you a question anyway."

"Shoot." He took a long drink from his mug.

"Do you know her parents?"

"I've seen them around."

"They're obviously witches, but since they've done something to bind her powers and they aren't part of the coven, what's the story? Are they part of the shadow coven?"

Dad's eyes turned hard the way they did any time the shadow coven was mentioned. "I don't know. They aren't part of our coven, that's true, but it doesn't always mean they're part of another. Some people don't want the responsibility."

"But then they don't get the protection."

"That's true." He considered me for a moment before continuing. "I can ask around if you want me to."

Shaking my head, I began moving closer to my car. "Nah. I sent Luken a text asking him to reach out to Danna."

Dad snorted. "You're not a very good friend."

I gave him a wide grin as I opened the driver's-side door. "I'm the best friend."

After starting the engine, I patted the front pocket of my jeans to make sure the necklace was there. I'd checked a dozen times already, but this wasn't something I was going to mess up. Then I chuckled at the fact that even Dad knew about the awkwardness between Luken and Danna.

They weren't a love match. Honestly, the two of them could barely stand the other. But they also couldn't seem to stop seeing each other naked. Not a big deal in my book. Lots of people had friends with benefits.

But they weren't friends and there was only one benefit.

Those two left my mind when I pulled into

Hazel's driveway to see her sitting on the front step. I didn't need more than one guess as to why she was outside waiting for me and not inside where I'd have to knock on her door.

She was the picture of summer in another dress made of thin material. I knew without touching it. Thin straps and sandals wrapped around her feet like a hug. Her red hair was up in a bun with small pieces gently brushing her face in the wind.

Damn this woman was beautiful.

Hazel lifted her head and the tiniest of grins curved her full lips. She stood and grabbed the backpack on the step beside her.

Before I could get out of the car, she yanked the other door open and slid in.

"Good morning," she said, sounding far too awake.

"Morning." I leaned over, wrapped my hand around the back of her neck, then pulled her toward me so I could kiss her.

It wasn't the kind of kiss I wanted to give her, but it was appropriate for where we were. The last thing either of us needed was for her mom or dad to come out to find us groping each other.

As I pulled away, I slid my hand over hers and

threaded our fingers together. "Anywhere specific you want to get breakfast?"

"Actually… I was wondering if we could just grab bagels or donuts and head out to the lake. The day is already so beautiful."

"We can do whatever you want, baby." I gave her a grin and then took us to the bakery, where they had both bagels and donuts.

Twenty minutes later, the two of us were sitting on the dock over the water eating our donuts and sipping our drinks.

"So you're going to train me in witchy stuff." It wasn't a question, but she said it as she ripped off a piece of a chocolate-covered donut and popped it into her mouth.

"Well, first we're going to see if we can get something out of you."

"What's that mean?"

"See if we can get the magic you have to come out. Do something. Like… have you ever had something happen you couldn't explain? Maybe you were frustrated and something nearby fell."

Her deep-green eyes widened. "My gremlin!"

I stopped chewing to ask, "Your what?"

She quickly finished the bite she already had in

her mouth then took a drink of her pop. Once that was clear, she said, "My gremlin."

"I heard you the first time. I just don't understand it."

She snickered with a hand over her mouth. "I have thought that I have either a ghost or a gremlin for a while now. Because... for example, the other day, I was in a hurry and couldn't find my phone. A few weird things happened in my room and I thought it was a ghost or a gremlin. But from the sounds of it, it was me?"

That was a good sign. Her magic was trying to get out and my job had just gotten a lot easier.

"That's exactly it," I told her. "You were frustrated, and random things happened without you knowing how to channel your magic. We're going to work on channeling that frustration to control your magic."

"All right." She slid one hand over the other quickly, like she was brushing off whatever crumbs were left there. Then she stood. "Then let's do this."

I took one last bite and a quick drink, then quickly put everything back in my car so it wouldn't get full of ants or whatever other insects were crawling around and we could have more later after we'd worked up an appetite.

Now we were ready to do this.

"So you said that when things happened before, you were frustrated, right?" I confirmed. She nodded. "Well, think of some things that really frustrate you. Let's see what happens."

Hazel shook out her hands then closed her eyes and took a deep breath. Her face remained unchanged and I desperately wanted to know which frustration she was thinking about.

But nothing happened.

"Well that was anti-climactic," she said with an edge to her voice.

"Don't put yourself down," I told her. "It's a learning process. Let's get you grounded first."

I moved over until I was an arm's length away from her and took her hands in mine. "Close your eyes and take a deep breath." She paused but then did as I instructed. I didn't. I watched her. "Keep taking deep breaths and feel the earth beneath your feet. Visualize it as an extension of you. This is something that you'll eventually always do without thinking about it. Kick your shoes off."

She was wearing those flat slip-ons that women tended to like, which meant she could easily get them off without opening her eyes.

"Press your feet into the earth. Feel the energy

pour through you," I instructed. She wet her lips. "Do you feel it?"

"I feel something," she whispered and I wasn't sure if she meant the energy of the earth or me since I was standing there getting hard while barely touching her.

Pushing all the dirty thoughts aside, I pulled energy up from the ground myself. She'd have to feel it coming from me, if nothing else. The warmth of the energy flowed through my veins as I held back all of my magic. If I did it for her, she'd never learn.

"Think about the area around us," I whispered. "The grass, the flowers, anything. Think hard about what you might change or what you'd like to see." Her lips parted and her chest rose then fell rapidly.

"The flowers," she said quietly. "I wish the flowers weren't dying."

The heat of the summer was turning the grass brown and causing the flowers to wilt.

"Picture it in your head."

As soon as I'd told her to do that, the flowers around us sprung up like it was spring, opening to their full bloom and making everything beautiful.

I stepped closer to her. "Open your eyes."

She did, but at first, she focused on me. It wasn't

until I'd raised an eyebrow that she began to look around.

Her eyes widened and her lips parted. "Did I do that?"

"You did. Now I helped give you a boost of energy from the earth, but only so you'd know what it felt like."

"I did that?" Hazel swung her arms around her. "You didn't do that?"

I snorted. "No. I told you."

"I... I just... wow."

A deep chuckle rumbled my chest as I remembered the first time I'd done some simple magic. The feeling wasn't something I could describe if I wanted to. Overwhelming, sure. Amazing, absolutely. But there'd been something about it that had made me feel powerful and I hoped that Hazel was experiencing the same thing right now.

It was a simple draw from the earth, but it packed a huge punch.

"I can't believe I did that. What else can you teach me?"

A smile slowly slid over my face as I pulled her to me. "Everything."

Her breath caught. "I meant about magic."

"So did I."

She shook her head as she stepped out of my arms. "Let's do it again. I want to learn everything."

We spent the next few hours going over simple things she could do by drawing on the elements. I also explained that eventually, she was going to have to be touching the element she wanted to use and as we pulled more of her power out of her, she'd be able to do other things as well.

"Like what?" she asked. "What's the scariest thing you can do?"

I slowly released a breath. This might not be something she could handle. "The scary shit is more about the spells I know. I've just learned to channel everything really quickly without having to think about it too much."

"And I'll be able to do that?" I nodded. "Could you kill someone with magic?"

My chest tightened. I didn't really want to get into that right away, but if she was asking, I'd answer. "Yeah. I can. I don't like to, but there's a spell for it and my powers are more advanced than yours right now."

"Wait." She raised an eyebrow and took a step back. "You said you don't like to, which means you have?"

Fuck. "Yeah. I have. Honestly, most witches have

because there are threats to us all around. There's the shadow coven. There're sadistic humans. People who don't really understand what we do. Now, the general rule of the coven is we only act in defense for that shit. And I'd kill again right now if you were in danger."

Her eyebrows furrowed as she thought about what I'd said. "That will take some time to process, but you ended it with something kind of hot." I had no idea what she was talking about and it must've shown. "If I were in danger, you'd kill for me. That's some hot, protective alpha shit right there, Miller."

I snorted. "Witches don't have alphas. That's a shifter thing." Though I wasn't sure she was ready to hear about the other supernatural creatures that existed outside of paranormal romances.

Her face blanched as she shook her head. "I'm seriously going to ignore the shifter part of that statement, but I didn't mean 'alpha' as in 'leads the pack.'"

She was right about that. Where she was concerned, I'd burn the fucking world if it meant she'd be safe. And as far as I could tell, the biggest threat to her was her parents.

"So you could bring that bottle of water over

here without touching it if you wanted to?" she asked, almost like it was a challenge.

I grinned and shook my head. Then reached out my hand and the water bottle flew off the hood of my car and into my hand.

As I handed it to her, she looked up at me and said, "That's incredibly badass."

"Leave it to you to think one of the simplest things is badass."

She shrugged. "It's not something *I* can do."

"You will. We have to continue training and next up is spells. You're going to learn so many, you won't know how to handle them all, but we'll take it as slow as you need to."

"Good. I'm excited." She lifted the back of her hair off her neck.

The sun had grown incredibly warm as the day had worn on. We'd been out here for hours. Not only did we need a break, but we needed to cool off.

"Want to hop in the lake?" I asked her.

She tilted her head to the side. "You didn't tell me to bring a suit."

I scratched at my chin like I was confused. "I didn't, did I?"

"*Miller*." My name came out of her mouth like a warning.

As I backed away from her, I held my hands out to my sides. "After what you told me yesterday, I didn't think you needed a suit."

A sexy blush crept up her chest and neck until her cheeks were bright pink. "Miller."

I reached back with one hand and yanked my shirt over my head then quickly undid my pants and pushed them down. All of my clothes were dropped where I was as I kept backing up toward the lake.

Hazel's rapid breathing had a fantastic effect on her tits as I watched her battle herself to keep her eyes focused on my eyes. But I was completely naked and she wanted to look. Hell, *I* wanted her to. If I was walking around naked, there was a reason.

Just as she finally glanced down to where my half-hard cock was quickly becoming full, I turned and dove into the water. It was cool and refreshing against my hot skin but did nothing about the erection that I figured would be a constant as long as Hazel was around.

When I broke the surface, Hazel was on the end of the dock with her arms folded under her breasts. "You expect me to skinny-dip with you?"

"No," I told her honestly. "I don't expect anything. I was hot. Now I'm not."

"There are people right there." She pointed to the swimming side of the lake.

I scoffed. "Please. They can't see us. The other side of the lake is really far even if it doesn't look like it. I mean, see for yourself." She raised a brow. "OK, they can see us, but they can't *see* us. They know we're here, but not that I'm buck-ass naked."

At first, I thought she was going to stomp away and tell me I was an asshole. But she did exactly the opposite. She locked her gaze with mine then slid the straps of her sundress off her shoulders so that it floated to the dock. Then she pushed her white, cotton panties down her smooth legs.

Hazel was beautiful. Her red hair lay over her shoulders but wasn't long enough to cover her hardening nipples. Her breasts were a perfect handful. Exactly right for her proportions. Her hips curved into shapely legs that led to the promised land.

Fuck. She was about to kill me, but it'd be a glorious death. My one regret would be that I'd never gotten to be inside her.

Then she jumped.

Water splashed over me like someone had dumped water on a dog in heat, only for me, it didn't have the effect it was supposed to.

She finally surfaced and then swam within arm's-length of me.

"Surprised I jumped in?"

"Actually, no. You're pretty brave and I didn't think you'd back down from the challenge."

She used her hand like a scoop to throw water at me, which brought out a loud laugh. That was when I realized that I was standing, but she was treading water. Her height meant that she couldn't touch the bottom.

I slid a hand around her waist and pulled her to me. Her skin was hot against mine as her tits pushed into my chest.

"You're so fucking beautiful, Hazel," I told her once she'd stopped flailing in the water.

"You've already got me naked, Miller. You don't have to flatter me."

I caught her chin with my free hand. "I'm not. You're beautiful."

She wet her bottom lip then pushed hers against mine.

Hazel threaded her fingers into my wet hair as I slid both of my hands around to cup her ass and lift so she could wrap her legs around my waist.

I was so close to her entrance and more than hard enough to make it good for her, but I didn't want to fuck her in the water. Not the first time. I wanted a bed where I could take my time and she wasn't wrong. There were too many people across the lake for me to take her on the dock anyway.

It was fucking tempting, though.

Instead, as our tongues moved against each other, I held her ass with one hand and then took the other around the front of her to create room. Room for me to stroke her pussy and then circle her clit. She groaned into my mouth and loosened her legs, like she had all the faith in the world that I wouldn't drop her.

When I knew she was ready, I pushed one finger into her tight pussy then another as I pressed my thumb against her clit.

She dropped her head back and groaned.

"Ride my fingers," I told her.

She hesitated before moving her hips.

"Miller," she whispered like a prayer and I almost emptied myself right then.

This was even better than anything I'd imagined in high school.

I used my rhythm to push her over the edge so that she was coming on my fingers. Once she'd come down, she nuzzled her face into my neck as her body went limp. I thought that was it, but she reached in between us and grabbed my cock like she was going to slide it inside her. I grabbed her wrist so that she'd drop me and brought it up to my chest.

"But—" she protested.

"Why don't we go back to my apartment?"

Hazel's eyes were burning with desire as her chest rose and fell rapidly against the water. "I don't know if I can walk."

"I'll carry you."

She snickered as I carried her back to the dock so that we could both climb up. Watching her put her clothes back on was the opposite of what I wanted to do, but my priority was to get her back to my apartment and naked again as soon as possible.

12

———

HAZEL

Every touch of Miller's hand against me sent electricity racing through my body. From the feel of his erection nudging at me, he wanted me as much as I did him.

My legs were jelly, barely holding me up when I lifted myself onto the dock.

Miller watched with heated eyes as I put my clothes back on, but I purposefully didn't slide my panties on.

If he was going to work me up and then throw cold water on me so that we could get back to his apartment, then he was going to make that drive knowing that I was bare under my dress. After scooping up my shoes, I marched toward his car.

He had to run after me as he pulled his shirt over

his head, though he quickly slipped his shoes on before sliding in behind the wheel.

"Did you leave your panties off?" he asked as he brought the engine to life.

"Sure did," I told him. The wheels on the car spun as he hit the gas, bringing a giggle from my chest.

"You're killing me."

"Me?" I asked. He slid his hand up my thigh, but not high enough to touch me like I wanted him to again. "*You're* the tease."

He grunted but kept driving too fast until we were in the driveway of his parents' house. My hair was clinging to the sides of my face and I did my best to make it presentable but I only had my fingers. My clothes were also pasted against the seat and I began to wonder how much damage we were doing to the seats of his car.

"Uh... no," I told him. "You said 'apartment,' not your parents' house."

"Please." He scoffed then hopped out of the car, so I did the same. "I live in the apartment above the garage."

Well, that was better. Here I'd had the fleeting thought that he'd intended to take me into his parents' house, which wasn't something I'd be comfortable with. We weren't kids anymore and that wasn't how I wanted to meet his parents the first time.

He took my hand in his and then hurried us up the stairs. My toe caught on the step as I stumbled my way up. He was as impatient as I felt.

Once inside, Miller pushed me back against the closed door, boxing me in with his arms. He leaned down and claimed my lips, his tongue sliding over them until they opened.

His hand dropped to my thigh and then slid up until he could cup my bare ass. It hadn't been long since I'd gotten out of that lake, but with the heat, it'd been enough to dry me off. My clothes were slightly damp, as was my hair, but they weren't dripping.

"Fuck, Hazel," he whispered against my mouth.

"What?"

"You're so fucking beautiful."

Goosebumps exploded across my skin. "You know how to make a girl feel good about herself."

"You are," he said, then he kissed me again. "You always have been."

I threaded my fingers through his hair and then brought his mouth back to mine.

We were a ball of raging hormones and

emotions. I pushed against his shirt so that he'd take it off and give me access to all that skin. I kissed down his neck, then chest, until I dropped to my knees. My fingers found the button holding his jeans up and popped it. With the denim being wet, I needed his help getting them off.

As he did that, his erection tapped against my chin. I locked eyes with him, stuck my tongue out, and licked him from the bottom to the tip.

"Fuck," he hissed as he braced a hand on the door.

I had no idea what his place looked like because all I could see was Miller and honestly, I didn't care. It'd been too long since I'd been with anyone and this was Miller. If when this was all said and done, he wanted nothing to do with me, I wouldn't even care.

This right here would be worth it.

He threaded his fingers in my hair with a firm grip and then pulled back so that he'd fall from my mouth.

"Fuck, Hazel." He was as breathless as I felt.

Need took over.

Miller reached down, wrapping his hands behind my thighs, and lifted. My legs wrapped around his waist automatically. I didn't have to think about it.

He carried me over to the bed but set me on the edge, even though I'd assumed he'd want me in the middle.

I was aching for him to be inside me, but instead, he pulled me even closer to the edge as he dropped to his knees. He spread my legs with his shoulders and wrapped his big hands around my thighs.

My stomach exploded with a swarm of butterflies in anticipation of his next move.

"Miller. You don't have to—" My words were cut off when he kissed the sensitive area between my legs.

He'd already given me an orgasm at the lake. I would've been fine if he'd just wanted to get to it. But hell, this felt good.

"You think I'm going to have you naked on my bed and not get a taste?" He made a noise in his throat that told me I was crazy.

Then he went back to work.

He pushed my legs up, causing me to fall back against the bed, and I didn't want to know why he was so damn good at this.

He sucked my clit into his mouth and I was

surprised I didn't come undone right then. When he pushed two fingers into me, I knew I was done for.

The change from sucking to licking then back again paired with his fingers pistoning back and forth had the pleasure building. He licked from the bottom of my pussy back to my clit then sucked it into his mouth.

That was all I needed. Even though he'd already made me cum at the lake, my muscles tensed and the eruption took over. The noises coming from my mouth were embarrassing, so I slapped a hand over it.

It wasn't until I came back down that he removed the hand.

"Next time, I want to hear all of that."

I opened my eyes just a slit in time to see him wipe the back of his hand over his mouth and I could feel the blush on my chest. It wouldn't be long before a red flush was everywhere.

Damn, being a redhead had its drawbacks.

"You shy?" he asked with a playful tone.

"Shut up." But I didn't look at him.

"Hey." He took my chin between his finger and thumb to turn it toward him. He didn't say another word until I opened my eyes and I pretended to not know that his fingers were now sliding through the curls between my legs. "There's nothing to be embarrassed about."

"I'm not."

"You're blushing."

I groaned. "Telling me that just makes it worse." And sure enough, the heat now spread to my cheeks.

"That rosy tone is beautiful on you."

I bit my lips together and shook my head. "I'm not embarrassed."

"Good," he said as he kissed his way up my shoulder and neck. "Because I could eat you all day," he whispered right into my ear.

And *now* I was embarrassed.

No one had ever talked like that around me. Most likely because those people were part of my parents' world and would get my father's wrath if they did anything like Miller just had or spoke the way he had.

Miller urged me up the bed so that there would be enough room for him then he settled between my legs, pushing his erection through my folds, but not into me. Yet it still hit a glorious spot.

Feeling bold, I pulled him closer, kissing him, tasting a little of myself on his lips.

Being with Miller was all about crossing lines I'd never crossed before and I was loving it.

Threading my arm between us, I didn't stop until I had a hold of his erection so that I could put it at my entrance myself.

"Uh…" he started, but I kissed away any of the words he was about to say.

He hesitated and it took far too long for me to realize why. We were about to have sex and there'd been no talk about condoms or any kind of safety. Another first for me.

"I have an IUD," I told him. "But you can get a condom if you want to."

The last word came out more like a yell. Before I'd finished my sentence, Miller pushed into me, balls deep with one stroke, which caused me to arch my back against the invasion. It was a welcome invasion, but a surprise, nonetheless.

"Damn, you feel so good," he murmured against my skin before he gently bit the swell of my breast.

It wasn't hard, but I marked up like a peach, so I'd probably have another reminder of him on my body tomorrow.

He pumped in and then out of me as I ran my fingers up his back and threaded them into his hair there. The room filled with sounds of our pleasure. Then a squeal as he rolled us over without warning.

I was on top of him. A position I'd never truly been comfortable with.

"I—I don't know what I'm doing." I'd only been on top once or twice and it'd been brief because I'd had no idea what I was doing. I wasn't playing shy with Miller, but I wanted to make him feel as good as he made me feel and I didn't think this would be the way.

"Just move your hips," he said, gently gripping them with his big hands. "Like this."

Back and forth, he urged me, hitting a completely different spot from this angle that felt so good, I almost forgot that I wasn't experienced at this part. I moved in whatever way felt good as his hands cupped my breasts.

Then I placed both of my feet flat on the bed so I could raise the drop myself. Miller cursed and moaned and grabbed me roughly by the back of the neck to bring me to him for a kiss. His hips met mine as he thrust up when I dropped down. Any harder and it would've hurt, but he seemed to have found the sweet spot.

My legs began to shake as we kept going, but he surprised me again by flipping us back over. The relief was brief as my pleasure began to build again.

This time, when I came, he was right there with

me. His grunt as he released inside me should've sounded ridiculous, but it wasn't. It was the sound of him at the height of his pleasure and immediately, I wanted to hear it again.

Miller dropped his forehead to my collarbone with all of his weight on top of me. He was like a deflated balloon that couldn't move on his own.

"Miller." The words were strained due to my lack of oxygen. "Miller, I can't breathe."

He pushed up onto his hands, taking the pressure off. "Sorry." He kissed me again. "I think I might've passed out."

I furrowed my brows. "*Passed out?*"

"That was fucking amazing. Off the charts."

I snorted and shook my head, but he rolled off so I could go use the restroom. When I came back, he did the same thing and then found me under his sheets when he was done.

Miller snuggled right into me and this right here was the most comfortable I'd ever been in my life. Not just after sex. Ever.

He kissed along the path from my shoulder to my neck as we lay there with my back to his front and my ass in his lap. Now was usually the awkward part. What do you say to someone after you had sex with them?

In the past, it had been easy. We'd just kind of awkwardly made excuses to leave. But I didn't think that would cut it with Miller.

"So..." I dragged the word out.

"Yeah, no shit."

Though I didn't know what he thought I'd said, I took it as a good sign.

"I have something for you," he murmured against my hair.

"If it involves me getting out of this bed, I don't think I can right now."

He snickered as he kissed my temple. "I'll bring it to you."

While he got out of bed, I stretched my entire body, which reminded me that there were muscles I hadn't used in a while and I'd probably be feeling it tomorrow. A small smile appeared at the idea of being reminded of Miller tomorrow when we probably wouldn't be together. I wasn't deluded into thinking that I got to monopolize his time just because we'd had sex.

Were we even in a relationship? Hell, I didn't know.

"I made this for you," he said as he slid back in beside me.

I flung myself up as if I had some newfound

energy. More than I'd had a minute ago anyway. "Made?"

He shrugged. "Well, we had the necklace, but Oliver and Luken helped me spell it."

I furrowed my brows. For a few brief moments, I'd forgotten about the whole witch thing. Miller had that effect on me, but now that I was thinking about it again, I realized that I'd actually made things happen at the lake.

I still didn't really know how to use any of my magic, but it was there. He'd proven that and now I wanted to learn everything.

Finally, I found his eyes. "'Spell it'?"

"Yeah. It's a talisman of sorts. Really, a protection amulet."

"Whom do you think I need to be protected from?"

He scratched at the back of his head. "Your parents."

I rolled my eyes. "My parents are selfish assholes, but they aren't going to hurt me. That wouldn't fit in with their plan to bring me into their world."

"That's what I'm afraid of," he said softly. When I didn't understand, he continued. "It's not just them, but you're new to being a witch and have a lot of learning to do. That makes you an easy target."

Ignoring the fact that he'd called me an "easy target," I asked. "For?"

"The shadow coven. Your parents. Hell, anyone looking to take advantage of a fledgling witch."

While trying not to let his words hurt, the idea that he thought me so helpless stung. He wasn't saying anything to be mean, but damn. My parents had always told me that they thought I was naive to the world and someone was going to take advantage of me. Hell, they'd probably think that was what Miller had just done.

"OK," I finally told him.

"You'll wear it all the time?"

I nodded and slipped the necklace over my head. "Everywhere but the shower." His scowl said that wasn't the right answer. "Er... Everywhere, including the shower?"

"That's better."

He pulled me into his arms and then laid us down again. When his hand slid across my stomach and then nudged my legs apart, I was happy about where this was going. Again. Because I didn't think I'd ever get enough of Miller Campbell.

But now there was a whole new set of worries.

There was a danger to me out there and I might've been living with them.

13

MILLER

The council had picked the wrong man to train Hazel.

There was no way around that.

It was too hard to be in her space and not touch her. Like when I brought her to my house to show her the potion room since apparently she couldn't visualize it as I'd explained it. I'd been standing behind her with my arms reaching in front of her, but her soft skin had been too much for me to pass up. Just that position had led to me kissing up her neck while she'd tried to get me back on track.

She'd learned nothing and to be honest, that was me failing.

Failing because it was my job to make sure she could protect herself and not only because the council had ordered me to. If something happened to her and I could've shown her how to stop it and hadn't because I'd been too busy thinking with my dick, I'd never be able to live with myself.

I needed to get it together.

So I spent a week keeping it in my pants and teaching her everything I could, no matter how much she tried to tempt me into something more. She was a natural talent. One that meant we could move quickly and after just a few days, she was able to do spells without saying them out loud.

It might not have sounded like much, but there were far more trained witches who couldn't even do that.

Each time she mastered something, I pushed ahead.

Which was why we were in the clearing where Luken, Oliver, and I had dispatched a few of the shadow coven witches recently. It was a secluded place to practice.

"No way," she told me with her hands on her hips. She was wearing a tank top with jean shorts because I'd told her not to wear the dresses she was so fond of. If we were training—I mean, *really* training—then she could have her skirt flying all around her. Not to mention there was no way I wanted Luken or Oliver to see what she had under the dress.

"It'll be OK," I told her.

"No." She wrapped her hand around the amulet I'd given her that day at my apartment. "You told me not to take it off. That it would protect me."

"You don't need to be protected here," I explained. "We're not going to hurt you."

"Or we're going to *try* not to anyway," Oliver added, which got him a glare from me.

"No one's going to hurt you," I repeated more for him than for Hazel. "But if you're wearing that, then you won't even have to try against us."

She cocked her head to the side in confusion. "Huh?"

"You can rely on the amulet to protect you. Even from us. Which means you won't know if what you're doing is working or not. If you cast a spell to counter one of ours, was it you? Or was it the amulet?"

"I can see what you're saying, but—"

I stepped into her space. "Baby, none of us are going to hurt you. None of our spells are ones that can hurt you. Not really."

"And if anyone else shows up," Luken told her, "we've got you."

She glanced at Luken and Oliver before finally nodding. After she'd slipped the necklace off her neck, she held it out to me. I couldn't be holding it, either, so I put it in the backpack we had sitting nearby. We'd brought water and snacks since no one had any idea how long we'd be out here.

Hazel moved to the middle so that the three of us could surround her.

"OK," I began. "We talked about the spells and you have a bunch of them memorized. You're further ahead than these two fools were when they first started."

"Excuse me?" Oliver countered. "You and I learned at the same time."

I shrugged. "I was better than you."

Oliver lifted his middle finger and stretched it out as far as it would go in my direction. Hazel's snicker reminded me that she was off guard right now.

"I'm ready," she told me with a curt nod.

I threw an easy warming spell her way, which she blocked expertly. The other two began to do the same. Hazel threw up a magical shield, which meant none of us were getting through. Except that I knew a counter. These spells were all harmless, but ones that she would've felt hit her if they had. It was impressive, but my girl was getting tired. Her reflexes were slowing.

Then she yelled, "Ouch!" and cradled her shoulder.

"What happened?" I asked as I ran over to her.

"I don't know, but it felt like... lightning," she said. "I don't know what lightning feels like and it's probably worse than this, but damn, that hurt."

"Damn it, Oliver," I snapped before stomping my way toward him.

He held his hands up like he was an innocent in all of this. "What? It wasn't going to hurt her."

I stopped when we were toe to toe. "Really? Because she just said it hurt."

He shook his head. "It smarted at best. These are harmless spells we were casting and she needs to know how to handle ones that aren't. If the shadow coven got a hold of her..." He shook his head. "She'd be toast."

"I'm going to rip your throat out."

"Whoa." Luken slid in between us. "That might be an overreaction."

"I told her we wouldn't hurt her!" I yelled, not backing down from the two of them.

"Bro, you need to calm down," Oliver said after

he took a couple of steps back. "It didn't hurt her. She's fine."

"He's right." Luken pointed behind me.

When I turned, I found Hazel standing there with her mouth dropped open and her eyes wide. *Shit.* I was probably scaring her.

"We're going to go," Luken told me, but I'd already begun walking away from them.

"I'm sorry about that," I said once I was closer. "Your shoulder OK?"

"Yeah." She rubbed it once more then dropped her hand. "It wasn't that bad." She took a breath then wet her lips. "Your reaction, however... "

"Yeah. Sorry about that."

She walked over to the backpack and took out a bottle of water. "Oliver may never speak to you again."

"Nah. We'll be fine. We've fought worse than that before."

"Men make no sense," she said before taking a sip. Couldn't argue with that. "I better get home anyway. I have to shower and I work closing tonight."

"Yeah. OK."

The first thing I did was put the amulet back over her head because if I wasn't with her, she needed that for protection. At least it was something I could do.

I'd picked Hazel up to go do the training, so I dropped her off and then headed home. But I didn't go into my apartment. Instead, I headed into my parents' house. It was Saturday, so they probably should've been home.

Before I could get into the house, Danna called and I was summoned to the council. Not what I wanted to do with my day. On my way, I called Luken and Oliver, who said they'd meet me there.

Danna led me into the meeting room where the council sat and I took my seat in the middle of the room. It always felt like an interrogation.

"We've called you here, Miller, because we've gotten some news," Danna told me. It was odd that Michael was letting her do the talking. "The shadow coven has stepped up their game and is calling in their witches. At least as far as we can tell."

"OK. I'm not one of them, so why was I called in?"

"Well..." She took a beat, then her eyes met mine. "We aren't one hundred percent sure yet, but our information says that Hazel's parents are in the hot seat right now. That they are part of the coven and the pressure is coming down on them to get their daughter to make the choice."

Fuck. Fuck. Fuck.

This news what we'd been expecting but fucking hell I had wished it was anything else. Those two with Hazel under their roof put her in danger and if her parents were under pressure, that was going to trickle down to her.

"How is training coming?" Michael asked.

"She's good. She catches on quickly."

Michael snorted and while I couldn't explain it, I didn't like the tone.

"So our intel says that the shadow witches have something big up their sleeves that we haven't discovered yet." Danna ruffled through a few papers. "And that they're likely to make a move on any witches whom they view as 'theirs' being resistant to the choice."

"Why can't Hazel choose light right now? I'm sure she would."

"You know the rules, Miller," Danna reminded me. "You know that she needs to be at her full power to make that choice. The problem is that dark magic doesn't require the same thing. They have some sort of training they require before making the choice, but that's all we know."

"So you want me to do what? Take Oliver and Luken and track the shadow coven down? Didn't we just kill a few of them for you?"

"You did." Michael didn't need to raise his voice to be heard. There was power behind it. The kind that I couldn't fully sense and that was why I figured he led the council. All I knew about him was that my parents had met him right after I'd been born and had brought him into the coven. But I'd never been told that they'd remained friends.

It was weird and there was more to it, but my parents never gave up anything they didn't want to.

Danna cleared her throat. "We think that Hazel's parents are going to be the key. They can't force her —we all know that—but we think they're going to put more pressure on her than they already are. Are you confident she wants nothing to do with the shadow coven?"

"Yeah. I'm confident."

"Then she should be able to resist them. Does she have a protection amulet?"

"Of course."

"OK." Danna let out a breath, like she'd been holding it in anticipation of what I'd been going to say. "Then she should be fine for now, but we need you to keep a close eye on her and get any further information you can. We'd like to do a preemptive strike, but we need more information, like what this big thing they have planned is. Stuff like that."

"Got it. Is that all?"

"It is." She gave me a nod, which meant that I could go.

Luken and Oliver were both leaning against Oliver's car in the parking lot right in front of the building when I came out.

"What'd they say?" Oliver asked, but I scowled at him. I wasn't over him zapping my girl like he had earlier, but they needed this information.

So I went over everything Danna and Michael had said. No one had told me I couldn't.

"Damn," Luken muttered. "So they think she's a target?"

"Seems like they know she is." Oliver held his hands up when my jaw tightened. "Brother, it's not me you have a problem with."

"Maybe a little bit of a problem."

"Nah." He shook that notion off. "I did you both a favor and you know it. But you also know that Luken and I aren't going to let anything happen to her, either. Not if we can help it."

"Where is she?" Luken asked.

"Work. She closes tonight. I'll go there before she

finishes, but if I go now, she's going to murder me with her bare hands."

"She'll think you're babysitting her."

"Exactly." Which meant I was going home. After Luken had said he'd go by and put a protection spell on the store. Those didn't work the best when it came to whole buildings, but it was another layer of protection. Oliver agreed that he'd go by the bookstore every so often to make sure things were OK. Luken would too. Which meant I could go home for a little while anyway.

Mom was in the kitchen, leaning on the counter with her phone in her hand when I came in the back door. She glanced up and raised her eyebrows. "Fun day?"

"Yup." I made an exaggerated pop on the 'P.'

"Cooper," she called out. "I think your son needs his father."

Seconds later, Dad came into the kitchen.

"What's wrong?" he asked.

I furrowed my brows. "Nothing. Why do you think there's something wrong?"

Dad gave me a look then grabbed two bottles of beer out of the fridge before nodding his head toward the back yard. With the flick of his hand, he started a fire in the pit back there then motioned for me to take a seat.

The beer is refreshing though I wasn't sure I understood the fire. The sun had started to set, but the air hadn't cooled yet. A lot of the time in Michigan, the lake air blew off the water and chilled the night. Even when it was balls hot during the day.

"So what's going on?" he asked.

"Nothing. I told Mom nothing."

"She didn't believe you and you know she can tell these things."

I sighed. Mom wasn't a seer, but she did have some kind of sixth sense about things that always turned out to be true.

"I may have overreacted to something Oliver did," I told him, then I went on to explain what had happened when we'd been working with Hazel. "It was dumb."

"Sounds like it."

I gave him a sour look as I took another pull from my beer. "I couldn't help it," I said in my defense. "She got hurt and I... I don't know. Lost it."

"Yeah, it's hard." He turned his bottle in a circle with one hand. Dad was as easygoing as they came. I'd only seen him truly angry a few times and all of them had involved worrying about my mom. I mean,

I knew they loved each other, but my overreaction was nothing compared to his if he thought Mom was in any kind of danger or trouble.

It must have been hereditary.

"What's hard?" I asked.

"Having your heart walking around outside of your body, sometimes alone, knowing the dangers out there and that you didn't do all you could to protect her."

I swallowed hard. "What?"

He shrugged. "Your feelings for Hazel aren't a secret. Or if they're supposed to be, you do a shitty job of hiding them. You always did. How that girl didn't know you were hopelessly in love with her in high school, I've got no idea."

I snorted. "You're cracked, old man. I hid my feelings just fine."

"Yeah, OK." He didn't believe a word I said when it came to Hazel. Never had.

"Are you saying you haven't protected Mom?" That couldn't have been the case because that man hovered so much that it drove her crazy.

"There was one time and I vowed to never let it happen again. And it hasn't."

"What're you talking about?"

He shook his head. "That's not a story for now."

"Then when? I *am* grown now."

Dad snorted. "You're still a kid."

I wanted to argue with him but decided against it. Mom had always said that no matter how grown up I got, she'd still look at me and see the baby she'd held in her arms the night I'd been born.

"Anyway," he continued, "just tell her how you feel and that you're going to basically be a stalker until you know she's safe."

"I don't think that'll work."

"You'll figure it out, but you probably should apologize to Oliver in the meantime. He did you a favor."

"Why do people keep saying that?"

"Because he did something to protect your girl that you wouldn't have done. It sounds like Hazel was a little too comfortable knowing that nothing you three were doing could hurt her. That makes people complacent. She doesn't understand just how dark our magic can get." He waved his hand in the air, like he was brushing off his next sentence. "What Oliver did was show her that it can hurt her. And he did it without actually hurting her. That's a real friend."

Well, fuck.

Apologizing wasn't my favorite thing to do in the world, but deep down, I knew my dad was right.

All this time, I'd told myself that I'd been training Hazel the way I had Luken and that was bullshit. I'd been handling her with kid gloves and not really fully preparing her because I couldn't stand the idea of hurting her.

With Luken, I'd thrown every non-lethal thing I'd known and then some at him to put him on defense.

That was what Hazel needed.

I needed to scare her to protect her.

14

HAZEL

If parricide were a viable option that wouldn't lead to prison, I would've done it already.

It was like my parents somehow knew that I'd found out I was a witch and was working with Miller to figure out the craft and whatever powers I had.

Me seeing Miller wasn't a secret at this point. No, I hadn't told them myself, but it wouldn't have been surprising if someone in town had told them. Actually, if one of their *friends* had seen me with him, they'd probably have broken a leg running to tell my parents.

Small towns had their issues.

I was getting ready for work when the email came in. The one from a job in the city that I'd applied to. The interview had been weeks ago, right before Miller had shown up at the bookstore, so I'd written it off. But apparently, the hiring manager had gotten sick, so everything had been delayed.

Now they want to offer me the job.

This was what I'd wanted a few weeks ago. But was this what I wanted now?

My entire life had changed drastically since that interview. Did I now want to stay because of Miller? Or was it not because of Miller and more about being a freaking witch?

I was so confused.

With that confusion, I needed time. I sent them an email thanking them for the offer and asked if I could have a bit of time to consider it. That was the best I could do with no notice. I had a lot going on right now and a big move might not be the best thing for me.

Plus, there was Miller. I'd have to talk it all over with him as well because losing him to move to the city wasn't something I was looking forward to.

Hell, at the rate I was falling for him—or had already fallen, who knew—I didn't think the job in the city was going to work out at all. I'd still have school there, but if I moved and worked there, too, Miller and I would have to try long-distance.

But those were all things for later. Right now, I

needed to get my ass to work. Being surrounded by books for a few hours felt like the thing I needed right now.

Unfortunately, my parents were in the kitchen as I made my way through.

"Good morning, Hazel," Mom said with an unusually chipper tone.

With hesitation, I answered, "Good morning."

"You're working today?" Dad asked before taking a drink of his coffee.

I furrowed my brows. They were never interested in my day. "Yup."

"Are you seeing Miller after?"

Yup. One of their friends had told them.

"I'm not sure. We didn't make any plans." Then I waited for the other shoe to drop.

Dad cleared his throat. "We don't think seeing him is a good idea."

I rolled my eyes and opened my mouth to respond, but my mother butted in instead. "We're just saying that there are a lot of nice, young men at our gatherings. If you came, you might find someone more appropriate."

"What makes you think Miller's not a 'nice, young man'?"

Dad growled under his breath the way he had

my whole life if he felt I was missing something blatantly obvious. I had my amulet tucked into my shirt so neither of them would see it, but I was suddenly glad that it was there.

"No one's saying he isn't." She gave Dad a hard look. "But he's not... Well, his family just isn't..."

"Rich?"

"Yes." She snapped her fingers as if I'd hit the nail on the head. "He's in a different circle. That doesn't mean he's not perfectly nice. He's just not appropriate for our daughter."

Yeah, this was weird. I'd always known that my parents were snobs, but admitting it so freely wasn't something they'd done before. It made me think that they had something else up their sleeves and even if they wanted me in some shadow coven— which I still wasn't totally convinced of—being this nice to me wasn't going to work and they had to know it.

Sure at least one of them was a witch if I was but the shadow coven stuff? I wasn't buying it.

"You know that makes you both assholes, right?"

My dad's fist slammed down on the counter, causing both my mother and me to jump. "I'm not going to stand for that kind of language in my house."

"But it does. You're making it sound like you think Miller and his family are beneath you because they don't have the kind of money Dad does."

"No, honey," Mom countered, her honey-sweet tone back again, "I think your father and I would just feel better if you came to a function to see what else is out there. I know you had a crush on Miller in high school, but those days are gone. You can't let a silly high school crush determine your future. We want you on the right path." She stepped closer to me. "Even if we haven't always gone about it the right way, everything we want really is for you."

Yeah. I wasn't going to fall for that, but I needed to get out of this insanity and get to work.

"I've got to go."

As my fingers curled around the doorknob, my mother called out, "Just think about it, will you? One function to see what's out there and if he's still the one you want, we'll try not to stand in your way."

I shook my head then said, "Fine. I'll think about it."

But I was, in fact, not going to think about it at all. I didn't need to see other men to know whom I wanted. And I'd forgotten my reusable water bottle, so I turned back.

My father's words kept me from opening the

door, his voice carried, and there was no way he knew I was there.

"It's not going to work," he said, presumably to my mother.

"I know," she agreed. "But I'm not sure what else to do."

There was a moment where they were silent and I was trying to decide if I should keep listening or say screw the water bottle and get to work. But something inside told me that they were talking about me.

"You know what we need to do."

"I just think that's a little drastic."

"You know what we need to do," he repeated.

Mom sighed and said, "Fine. Let's get it set up, but I don't want her hurt."

That was when I noped the fuck out of there. They had to be talking about me and I didn't want them to know that I was still there.

Work was going to be hard to focus on because my brain would want to figure out what they were going to do.

Being strict assholes hadn't worked for them.

Being naive wasn't going to work.

What was left?

Four hours later, Miller came walking into the

bookstore. We'd just had a small rush, so his timing couldn't have been better.

"You get a lunch break?" he asked, glancing around at the other two people working today. The wrinkle between his forehead and the tense way he was carrying himself showed his concern. But I wasn't sure why it was there. "Or dinner? Whatever."

"Yeah. I'm actually due right now."

"You want to go somewhere?"

For the first time today, I gave someone a genuine smile. "Yes. But I have to eat because I'm starving."

"'I'll feed you," he said, shoving his hands into his pockets.

It must've been the day for weirdness because just as my parents had been this morning, Miller was acting weird. It was in a different way, but it was still weird.

After letting my coworkers know I was taking my hour-long break, I grabbed my purse and met him back out front. He wrapped an arm around my shoulders to lead me from the building to his car. I was craving a sandwich, so after a stop at the deli, he took us to the park, where we spread out a blanket.

The day was warm and sunny. The shade from

the big tree we'd settled near dropped the temperature several degrees. Then we dove in.

"Hungry?" he asked, a smile playing on his lips after I took my first bite.

I chewed quickly so I could answer him. "Yes. I didn't eat breakfast this morning. I was going to grab something on the way out, but my parents were being weirder than normal."

His back straightened. "What do you mean?"

I shrugged. "I don't know. They were being nice and to most people, it doesn't seem weird, but I swear for them, it is."

His brows furrowed and he dropped his sandwich back onto the paper it had been wrapped in. "That's part of the reason I wanted to have lunch today." He took a quick drink of his water. "I was called into the council. Something is going on with the shadow coven. Looks like they're calling their witches in and I don't know what all that entails, but the council thinks your parents specifically are in the hot seat."

My stomach dropped and my hand paused halfway to my mouth. Suddenly, I wasn't as hungry. "What's that mean?"

"I don't really know. Maybe demands are being made on them. Or maybe they're being threatened with punishment because they haven't brought you in yet."

My stomach tightened. "Why can't I join your coven right now?"

"Unfortunately, we have more rules than the shadow coven. You're not at full power yet, which is my fault. And if you did it now, it'd be because of me. Not to mention being part of our coven doesn't magically save you from them."

I swallowed hard. "When I was leaving the house today, I forgot my water bottle," I told him while something close to fear churned in my stomach. "I didn't go in to get it because I could overhear my parents talking."

"What'd they say?"

"It might not have been about me." I shook my head. It couldn't have been about me. What if it was?

"Hazel?" he prodded gently.

I blew out a quick breath before telling him. "My mom and dad are planning something. I don't know what it is, but my dad kept telling my mom that she knew what needed to be done." My eyes locked with his. "But she said she doesn't want *her* hurt."

"'Her'?" he echoed. I nodded. "You know that's you, right?"

"It might not be."

He tilted his head to the side and looked at me like a parent did when the kid knew they'd done something wrong. I was wrong was what he was telling me. My parents' discussion had been all about me and I had no idea why I was specifically so important. Why not run off and do the dark magic thing without me? I wasn't as good at controlling the magic or casting spells as Miller or the guys.

"What am I supposed to do?" I asked him while trying not to let fear flood my voice. In all my life, I'd never thought my parents would actually hurt me and that was when I reminded myself that Mom didn't want me hurt, though Dad had zero reaction to that.

"For one, you're staying at my place tonight. I'm not letting you go home to who knows what," he said. I nodded because home was the last place I wanted to be anyway. "I'm going to talk to my parents about this and make sure Oliver and Luken are ready if we need them."

"The council?"

He thought about that for a second before shaking his head. "They're already on alert and if we need the coven, we'll call them too. My apartment has wards all over the place, as does my parents' house. Fuck, if we have to, we'll stay in my old room there."

I winced. "Won't your parents care if you have a woman in your room?"

He gave me a full belly laugh and he took an annoyingly long time catching his breath. "No, Hazel. I'm a grown-ass man. I assume they know I have sex, if that's what you're talking about, but we'd only be there if we need extra protection. My parents are kind of badasses."

"I'm not having sex at your parents' house."

"Didn't even cross my mind. But we're staying in my apartment, so..."

I snorted and shook my head. Leave it to Miller to be thinking with his small head instead of the big one at a time like this. Though he might've just been trying to take my mind off everything.

He scooted toward me and took me into his arms, a place where I actually felt safe and secure. Feeling like I was in danger was new to me and I had to say, zero out of ten stars. Do not recommend.

"Nothing's going to happen to you, Hazel. Oliver, Luken, and I are going to get you to full power so you can choose the light and defend against anything coming your way."

As he said the words, I believed him.

What I didn't believe was my ability to do any of the things that he was talking about.

We finished eating, though both of us just picked at the food. Our appetites seemed to have left during the conversation about my parents.

What I didn't tell him was that now, I was kind of determined to figure out my parents plans. How they intended to get me over to their side. If we knew, it would help fend them off. Don't get me wrong. I wasn't going to run off on my own and probably get myself killed or committed to the shadow coven. But that didn't mean I wouldn't try to figure it out.

For now, though, I had to finish work. Once we cleaned up our area at the park, Miller took me back to the bookstore.

"Luken put a protection charm on the store. It's not impenetrable because it's hard to do the whole building, but it should help."

"Were Oliver and Luken assigned to me too?"

"No." He ran a hand down my back as we sat in front of the store. "But with us, where one goes, we all go."

"They're good friends to you?"

"The best and they'll put themselves between you and anything because of it."

I took a deep breath. There were feelings I was

having that I hadn't been able to put into words yet. Didn't know if I ever could because I didn't understand the feelings myself.

Was it love? How in the hell would I know when the only person I'd ever loved was my best friend? This didn't feel like that and I'd kind of been avoiding talking to her for a while because I knew she wasn't going to approve of Miller and I definitely couldn't tell her about being a witch.

I'd never even really loved my own parents or had been given love by them.

I had no idea what I was doing, but for now, I'd ride the feeling out.

"I'll pick you up after work," he told me. When I went to protest, he held up a hand. "I'll bring one of the guys with me to drive your car to my place."

"I can just meet you there."

He shook his head. "No. I don't know what's going on and until I do, I don't want you off on your own. I'd come sit inside the bookstore until you close, but I don't think you'll let me."

"I won't. I'll be fine, Miller. Maybe my parents weren't talking about me. Maybe it was another witch in their coven." And I hoped my voice sounded more confident than I felt. Because they'd been talking about me. I just didn't want Miller to know how much that freaked me out.

"Still, I've got people around to make sure you're protected and I'm going to go talk to my parents and maybe Danna to see if they know what your parents are planning to convince you."

"OK."

He gave me a quick kiss before I hopped out of the car and headed inside. He didn't pull his car from the curb until I was inside the store.

MILLER

IT TOOK EVERY OUNCE OF STRENGTH INSIDE MY BODY to let Hazel walk into that bookstore. Then I had to find extra to pull away from the curb.

Leaving her there went against every urge in me, but I knew that Oliver and Luken weren't far and would be checking on her.

My first stop was Danna's house, hoping that she was done with the council for the night. It was somewhere near dinner time, but I knew they went late sometimes. Luckily, she was there.

"Miller," she said with a shit ton of surprise. "What're you doing here?"

"What're you guys not telling me?" I stood on her front porch with my hands hanging limply at the sides.

"What?"

"About Hazel. Don't tell me that you're not hiding something." Because the council rarely told people everything.

Grabbing my forearm, she pulled me toward her. "Come inside." She shut the door behind us. "We don't need the entire town listening in. What's this about?"

I filled her in on what Hazel had overheard her parents saying. While Danna tried to maintain neutral features, she might've forgotten that I'd always been able to read her like a book. Even a little twitch in the corner of her eye told me she was hiding something. I was never sure if reading people so well was a witch thing or if I was just observant.

"Damn," she muttered.

"See? I know you know something."

"Come on." She waved her hand so I'd follow her to the kitchen, where she grabbed a beer out of her fridge and offered me one. I declined because I wasn't going to take the chance of being even slightly impaired until I knew Hazel was safely away from her parents. "There are rumors."

"Of?"

She took a long drink. "I'm not supposed to tell anyone about this, Miller."

I folded my arms over my chest. "But you're going to tell me, right?"

She sighed. "Yes, but you can't let anyone know that I told you. There are things that happen in the council room that are supposed to be confidential."

"We'll address that bullshit later," I spat. She furrowed her brows. "The council asks us to do all kinds of shit for them yet doesn't give us all the information. That's bullshit."

"Michael thinks—"

"I'm beginning to think Michael is bullshit, too."

She snapped back, as if I'd actually slapped her. "Damn, Miller. What's going on with you?"

"I need to know about any information involving Hazel." Because I wasn't about to go into the nitty gritty of one man running the coven. Sure, we had a council, but everyone knew that Michael made all of the final decisions, yet no one could tell me why.

He hadn't been elected.

Hadn't been chosen.

As far as I'd ever heard, he'd shown up the day I was born and very quickly taken over the council.

"Well, this isn't about Hazel specifically, but the reason we called you in to train her was because of certain rumors. Now they're just rumors. We have no confirmation."

"Keep going."

"A witch we contacted out east said that she'd overheard a conversation about a shadow coven camp."

"Camp?"

She nodded. "What she heard was that children of shadow coven members who don't fall in line by the deadline are taken to a reeducation camp."

"Indoctrination camp?"

She nodded. "Sounded like it, but it's a camp parents can send their kids that will convince them that the shadow coven witches are the good guys and we're actually the bad guys. So they can have their little army."

"How long has this been going on?"

"She didn't hear that. But the deadlines are arbitrary and adult kids are sometimes *encouraged* to go."

"Encouraged how?"

"She didn't hear that, either."

"So the council got worried Hazel would be sent to one of those places." I dropped into a chair at the kitchen table.

"Yes. As well as some others we believe belong to the shadow coven. It's like they're amping up for a war. You know that light magic is stronger than dark. Unless..."

"Unless you get a light witch to turn dark."

"Exactly. They have both sides of the coin at their disposal and can use light magic for dark purposes."

"So we're going to need everyone we can if the shadow coven ever comes knocking."

She nodded as she slid into the seat across from me. "We may not wait for them to come to us and the council has already worked on coven alliances. We have the numbers if we need them, but until it's decided, we wanted to protect any potential light witches from turning dark."

"Why is Hazel a light witch? Her parents are dark, right?"

"They didn't go to the shadow coven until after she was born. Both of their entire lines come from light witches. She inherited the same kind of powers you and I did, but her parents were wooed later. Plus, you know that if you make the choice to go dark, that's not inherited. You have to be from the original line of dark magic."

"Kind of like our most powerful witches come from the Salem line and the Michigan line."

"Exactly. Miller, you can't tell anyone I told you all of this," she repeated. I gave her a look and she sighed. "OK, no one other than Luken and Oliver since I know you three tell each other everything."

Her cheeks pinked up at whatever was going through her head.

"Not quite *everything*. We don't tend to kiss and tell."

Her shoulder relaxed and it made me wonder what the hell had happened between Luken and Danna. He'd never told us, even if we'd all known they'd been hooking up for a while, but what the hell would make her blush at the thought of me knowing?

Neither of them would ever tell me, but fuck, I wanted to know.

Focus, Miller.

"Hazel's staying with me tonight and probably every night until this is settled. I'll go with her to get clothes when her parents aren't home because they'll get her over my dead body."

Danna swallowed hard. "I think they'd be more than happy with that arrangement."

I snorted as I stood. "Thanks for the information, Danna. No one will know it came from you."

She pushed to her feet as well. "I don't know how much it matters. There've been secret meetings between certain members of the council that the rest of us aren't allowed to know about." She shook her head and rubbed her arms, like she was cold. "This doesn't sit right with me."

"Let us know if you need anything. We've got your back."

She gave me a thankful smile and then walked me to the door.

I took a few minutes to swing by my parents' so they wouldn't be surprised when Hazel was suddenly living with me. I didn't hate the idea of that being permanent, either. Then I asked Oliver and Luken to meet me at the bookstore.

Once there, I filled them in on everything Danna had told me.

"That's fucked-up," Luken said once I'd finished.

"Something like that is probably the reason your mom bound your powers," I told him.

He shrugged. "Maybe."

"You know, a few years ago, I heard some of the elders talking," Oliver started. "I wasn't paying too much attention, so I only remember parts of it, but I swear they were talking about some of our covens' girls or young women being impregnated and taken."

"What?" I asked, not believing it. "How young were you? There's no way the coven could keep that a secret."

"I think they could," he countered.

"We'd remember people just disappearing."

"Not if it was before you were born." Luken ran a hand through his hair. "Before I got here, obviously."

"No way." My parents would've told me about that, even if the coven wasn't going to.

"Do we know of anyone who would've been around our ages back then who no one sees anymore?" Oliver asked and my heart plummeted to my stomach, beating like a racehorse there.

I knew of someone, but again, that just meant my dad would've said something. I thought.

"I do, but she just left town."

"Who?" Luken asked.

My jaw tightened as I wished I would've kept my mouth shut. "My dad has a sister. She left town before I was born."

"But she's visited?"

"No. I've never met her."

Realization crossed Luken's face, like my aunt not visiting meant all of that was real.

"Come on," I said. "You think the council would keep that from us?"

"I don't put anything past the council," Luken answered honestly.

He hadn't grown up in Echo Valley, so he

didn't know them like Oliver and I did. The council only ever wanted what was best for us. That's what we were told. Though more than one person said they missed Serena Goode. She'd been the head of the council before I'd been born, but when I'd been young, she'd left to raise her granddaughter away from Echo Valley after her daughter and son-in-law had been killed in an accident.

"They didn't tell us about this camp," Oliver pointed out. "I'm guessing you got that information from Danna."

"No, I didn't." I was compelled to say that after promising her I'd keep everything quiet. She'd known I'd tell the guys, but not that I'd out her. I was going to keep that promise.

Though saying it hadn't been her didn't make them believe it hadn't been.

"I'm going to do some digging," Oliver said.

"Me too. I'll see what else I can get out of Danna." Luken pushed to his feet.

"Are you ever going to tell us what's going on with the two of you?" I asked because there was nothing better to be doing right now than talking about Luken's love life.

"Nothing. We hook up sometimes. That's it."

"Yeah, well, she got red as fuck earlier when she thought you told us things about your hookups."

This cocky half-grin appeared on Luken's face. "I'm good at what I do."

"Fuck off," I said through a laugh. Once we'd settled down, I told him, "Thanks for hanging around tonight. I'm just going to wait for her to get off, then we're going to my place. Call if you need me."

"If you wait for her to get off," Luken began with a look that said I wasn't going to like what he said, "instead of getting her off yourself, she'll never blush at the idea of someone knowing what you do in the bedroom."

Oliver and I groaned at the same time. "Never had any complaints," I told him.

"That you know of."

I lifted my middle finger and thrust it directly into his face.

He chuckled and walked away with Oliver. Giving each other shit was what we did.

"Hey," I called out. "Can one of you drive Hazel's car to my place at some point?"

Oliver reached a hand up. "Just leave the keys on the seat."

Back in my car, I had the radio playing low as I

waited for Hazel to get out of work. Living in Echo Valley meant doing shit like leaving keys on the front seat of a car was something we could do. Crime wasn't a prolific here and the shadow coven wouldn't be looking to steal a car.

When I sent Hazel a text letting her know that I was out back, something in my car beeped.

Well, shit.

I slid my hand under the passenger seat and came up with her phone.

I wasn't going to look through it or anything. Had no reason to, but on her locked screen, there was a preview of an email with a subject line that made it so I couldn't *not* look. I'd seen her enter her passcode a million times, so I already knew that.

Once the email came up, anger coursed through me.

It was from some bookstore in the city telling her to take all the time she needed to make her decision, but that they thought she'd be a perfect fit for the position.

Hazel was going to leave Echo Valley.

Protecting her was going to be so much harder in the city and I hated the idea of her being even forty minutes away.

But her goal was to get away from her parents.

That wasn't something she'd kept secret.

Fuck. It felt like there was a brick sitting on my chest.

She could've fucking told me. I tightened my grip on the steering wheel and stewed in my own anger and fear until my beautiful redhead came out the back door.

Her coworkers were with her and they were laughing about something, but all I could think about was the fact that I was going to lose her to the city.

"Hey," she said, as if she didn't have a care in the world as she hopped into my passenger side seat.

"Put your keys on the front seat of your car," I snapped, my mood dark. Her brows furrowed. "Or give them to me and I'll do it."

She handed over her keys but was clearly confused at my tone. Or maybe it was why we were leaving her car key.

When I got back into the car, she asked, "Why are we leaving the key?"

I didn't answer her, preferring to make this ride in silence.

"Miller?"

Again, I kept my focus on the road for as long as I could.

"Miller! Why did we leave my keys in my car?"

I ground my teeth together. "So Oliver can bring it to my house." Even to my ears, my tone wasn't the friendliest.

"What's wrong, Miller?"

"Nothing."

"Clearly something. What happened since I last saw you?"

I pulled the car out of the parking lot to head to my house. "I found this."

She was surprised when I tossed her phone to her, but she caught it easily. It hadn't been out of anger and I hadn't thrown it. When she looked down, she realized what my problem was.

"I was going to tell you about that."

I shrugged, tightening my grip on the wheel.

"You're mad that I got offered a job?"

"No. I'm not mad. I'm worried. If you move to the city, it's going to be a lot harder to protect you and there's shit going on that you don't know about."

"Then tell me."

I pulled into the driveway and cut the engine. "Most of it's just rumor and I don't want you to worry until I know what's going on. But I want you to be safe."

She reached out and cupped my cheek. "I'm not

taking the job, Miller. I asked them for more time because with everything going on, I didn't want to deal with it. A few weeks ago? Yeah, I would've accepted, got out of here as soon as I could, and never looked back." She wet her lips. "Things are different now. Do you think I'm too stupid to live or something?"

"What?" My eyes widened. "No. Why would you ask that?"

"Because you seem to think I'm about to run off away from you with only an amulet to protect me when my parents are planning to force me into the shadow coven. That sounds pretty stupid to me."

I snorted. "We do have to recharge the amulet."

"And I'm not the best at these things yet, am I?"

"Which is also my fault."

"Maybe we should go inside and talk. I don't have any pajamas, ya know."

The corner of my mouth twitched. "Maybe that was part of my plan."

She giggled as she yanked the handle on the door.

We did need to talk and my apartment would sure as hell be more comfortable than the car.

Plus, I didn't hate the idea of her being naked in my bed tonight.

16

MILLER

"Want anything to drink?" I asked after dropping my keys onto the little table by the door.

"Yes, please." Hazel shuffled off to the couch and flopped down on it. That was the only way to describe what she'd done. Flop. Her shoes tumbled off her feet and onto the floor.

She didn't sit up until I came back over to her.

"Thank you." She took a long drink of water and then scooted over with her legs folded together in front of her. Her skirt pushed up her thighs, but not high enough for me to see the goods.

I set my bottle on the table and turned slightly so we'd be facing each other.

"Did you think I'd run off to the city without talking to you first?" she asked.

"Maybe."

"Miller, we're doing something here. I'm wouldn't do that. But I got that email and with everything going on and I didn't want to answer it right away." Her hand settled on my thigh. "I applied for that job to get the hell out of here when I thought there was nothing keeping me here. That's changed."

"Yeah?"

"Yes. Like I said, we're doing something here. Not to mention I'm a witch now. Apparently. I'm still not totally sure I'll be a good one, but you say I am, so I am."

"You will be." I reached over, cupping her cheek then leaning in to kiss her softly on the lips. "But that also reminds me. I'm going to let Luken and Oliver take over your training."

Her green eyes widened. "Why?"

"Because to really help you, I'd need to do things like Oliver did when he zapped you. I can't do that."

"It only hurt for a minute."

I shrugged. There was no way in hell I was going to do anything to make her uncomfortable. "Still can't do it. I'll be there, but they'll be better for this."

She threw her hands in the air and began pacing the room like she was trying to burn off extra energy.

"Then why did the council send you? If they'd be better?"

I ran my hand through my hair. "My guess is they knew how I felt about you in high school and figured I'd want to do everything to keep you safe."

"Then why can't you?"

"Because they didn't bet on how I feel about you now."

Her footsteps stopped and she turned to me, hands on her hips. "Are you saying that you *like*, like me?"

I snorted. "I am saying that." Which she knew. She just also wanted to harass me.

Hazel slowly came over to me and stepped between my legs so I could hold her at the waist and rest my forehead against her lower abdomen.

"Did I ever tell you that I love the fact that you wear so many dresses?" My eyes met hers and a smile played on her lips.

"No."

"I do. Want to know why?" I slid my hands slowly down her thighs then back up against her bare skin until I could cup the very bottom of her ass cheeks.

"I can guess why."

All thoughts of her leaving were gone the moment my skin had touched hers. Though the fact that for the briefest moment I'd thought that I'd be losing her was probably behind all of my movements. I wanted to possess her. Wanted to make her feel so good that she'd be reminded of me for days.

Desperately hoped she'd forget she ever wanted to leave town, even if her reasons for that were more than valid.

I pulled on Hazel until she was straddling me on the couch, then slid back and widened my legs, which forced hers to widen as well. Our tongues battled for control, but both of us were winning. Because of the thin straps on her dress, I was able to pull them down, exposing her breasts to the air.

Fuck, it killed me that she ran around without a bra on and every person out there could see when her nipples got hard. Because they were sure hard right now. I ran my thumbs over the eraser-sized areola as I kissed my way down her throat.

As I worked my mouth over her breasts, sucking each nipple into my mouth, I wrapped one hand around the back of her neck so I could hold her right where I wanted her, and the other slid up the inside of her thigh, barely touching her skin.

When I got to her panties, I easily pushed those aside so I could rub her pussy. I'd been thinking about her all day and this was exactly where we needed to be.

I ran my fingers over her lower lips, causing her to squirm. Then I circled her clit, causing her to bite down where my neck met my shoulder.

"Where do you want my fingers?" I whispered into her ear.

"Everywhere."

"Can't be everywhere at once, baby. Do you want them here?" I pressed against her clit again, causing her to groan. "Or here?" I slid one finger into her pussy.

Her entire body tightened as she let out a sound that could never have been taken for anything but pleasure.

"So here, then?" I slid my finger out then back in twice before adding a second finger. She was so wet and ready that I was having a hard time controlling myself.

It would've been easy to throw her down on this couch and fuck the hell out of her, but I wasn't going to do that. I was going to make her cum first.

"B-Both," she finally got out.

"Your wish is my command." I pushed my fingers into and out of her, pistoning like I would've if it were my cock and pressed my thumb against her clit.

"Miller." My name came out on a moan.

Soon, I wasn't moving my fingers. She was sliding herself up and down them herself.

Watching my girl take the pleasure that she deserved turned me the fuck on. I wanted her more than I ever had. The straps of her dress were hanging loosely near her elbows. Her skirt was covering both her and my hand. And I was rock fucking hard, ready to explode in my jeans.

Hazel began to tighten around my fingers and I knew what was coming. I pulled one of her nipples into my mouth and scraped my teeth over it as gently as I could.

She moaned and came all over me.

Even the car door outside didn't stop me from doing what I was doing. I assumed it was Oliver dropping off Hazel's car. He wouldn't knock. Not knowing that I was in here with her and everything that was likely going on.

Then the knock came and I knew he was asking to die.

At first, I ignored it, figuring he'd get the hint and leave. Then he knocked again.

But Hazel was lying against me with her head on my shoulder and my fingers still deep inside her.

After the third knock, she said, "Must be important." Then she slowly slid off me.

My fingers glistened. While she tried to right herself, I stuck them in my mouth to quickly clean them off.

Her mouth dropped open as she slid her dress back over her arms. "I can't believe you just did that."

"Would you rather I answer the door with your cum all over my fingers?" I scoffed and shook my head. "It could be my mother."

She slapped her hands over her face and mumbled into them, but I couldn't understand what she'd said. All I could do was chuckle as I made my way to the door.

When I pulled it open, murder must've been all over my face because Oliver's eyes widened.

"Why are you here?" I growled.

He glanced from me to Hazel, who was disheveled, sitting on the couch looking exactly like we'd been doing what we'd been doing. Humor played on his face while I silently promised to end him if he said anything to embarrass her.

"Here're Hazel's keys." He held up the keyring. I snatched it and dropped them on the table next to the door.

"You could've left them in the car."

"I could've." He focused back on me. "But I wanted you to know there was a guy hanging out near it at the bookstore. When he saw me, he took off. I guess I'm not his type."

"What'd he look like?" Hazel asked from behind me.

"Tall, dark hair, but it was dark in the back parking lot, so I couldn't get the best look at him."

"It's probably the guy my parents tried to set me up with," she explained. "He looked a little eager to make it work. Probably eager to please my parents."

Why was this the first I'd heard about it? Slowly, I turned to face her. "*What*?"

"Yeah. It was a while ago. I turned him down. Maybe he wanted to ask again."

"I tried to follow him," Oliver told me. "I didn't want to use my magic because I wasn't sure if he was there for Hazel, if he was a townsperson, you know. So I ended up losing him."

Yeah. We weren't supposed to use our magic unless absolutely necessary out where the regular folks could see.

"I get it. Thanks, Oliver."

He gave me a nod then disappeared down the

stairs. I shut the door and locked it before turning back to her.

"Why didn't you tell me? He's probably part of the shadow coven."

"Uh…" She stood and came right over to me. "Because it wasn't a big deal. I said *no* and that was it."

"Clearly, that wasn't it."

She shook her head. "Listen, we can argue about this or we can get naked and make each other feel really good."

Well, that wasn't a hard decision.

I scooped her up in my arms as she squealed and took her to my bed.

In seconds, we were both naked and exploring each other's bodies. My cock hadn't softened at all while Oliver had been here and if I didn't get inside her soon, I was going to explode all over her.

"On your knees," I commanded.

She hurried into position. I pushed her head down so that it was resting against the mattress and spread her knees, exposing everything to my hungry eyes. I ran a finger the entire length of her from her ass to her clit. Her back arched, but she didn't try to stop me.

Hazel trusted me. Knew I wasn't going to do

anything to hurt her or anything she didn't want. I wanted her ass too, but we hadn't talked about that yet, so I pushed my cock into her pussy instead.

She was so tight from this angle. Her legs began to shake as I pushed further in.

"Just relax," I instructed her. She took a deep breath as I felt all of her muscles release. Finally, I pushed past that last bit of resistance and the only sound in the room was the quiet sigh from her.

Then the slapping of our bodies replaced everything else. When I didn't think she could hold herself up anymore, I pulled out and flipped her onto her back. Her movements were slow. A clear indication that her muscles would be sore tomorrow and I was good with that. Any reminder of me inside her filled me with pride.

This time, I went slower. I pushed into her and kissed her until we were breathless. She ran her fingers up my back the way she knew that I liked and wrapped her legs around my waist.

I had her caged in with my arms, but I moved slower and after a few minutes, pulled her legs back down.

Something had changed. This wasn't just about need. It was about something else and I had a word for it, but I wasn't going to think about it. Instead, I kept going until she released again and I followed right after.

Hazel wasn't really moving when I got off of her, so I went into the bathroom for a wet cloth to come back and clean her up so she wouldn't have to move right away.

"You don't—" she started.

"Let me take care of you."

She bit her lips together and didn't fight me on it.

Once she was cleaned off, I went back into the bathroom, cleaned myself up, and came back to my girl curled in a ball on my bed.

"I don't have any pajamas," she said quietly as I settled in on the bed.

"We can sleep naked."

A moment of silence was followed by, "I really hate sleeping naked. What if there's a fire?"

I snorted. "How about one of my T-shirts, then?"

She nodded, so I got her a clean one out of the drawer. I was going to put it on her, but she snatched it out of my hand on her way to the bathroom.

After putting on a pair of pajama pants, I crawled back into bed and waited for her. If she didn't like sleeping naked, that might've meant she wouldn't like me sleeping naked, either. Which I didn't normally do anyway.

Finally, she was done and back beside me with her head on my shoulder and her leg across mine. She drew little patterns with her finger on my chest.

"I lied earlier, Hazel," I said into the darkness, breaking the comfortable silence between us. *Shit.* I hadn't even thought to see if she was still awake or not. "When I said that I like you. I lied." Her muscles tightened, like she was waiting for the next shoe to drop. "I mean sure, I do like you. But I love you, Hazel."

I thought the declaration would've taken away all the tension, but it didn't. She clasped the sides of my face and brought me down to hers. When our lips met, I hoped it was emotion driving it and not her way of avoiding the fact that I loved her.

In all my rambling thoughts, it had never occurred to me that I loved her, but she might not love me back.

17

———

HAZEL

"I have to go home."

I knew those weren't the words Miller wanted to hear the next morning, but they were words I had to say, nonetheless.

"I figured." Miller took a drink from his coffee cup. We were sitting at his small table after just finishing breakfast. He had to work today and so did I, which meant that I needed clean clothes and to take a shower.

Now, I could shower here, obviously, but the thought of putting already worn clothes back on wasn't appealing.

"Don't be grumpy about it. I need clothes."

"You could borrow some of my mom's."

I gave him a pointed look. "No, I can't. I need my

clothes. If you want me to pack a bag to stay here I will, but I need my things."

He glanced at his phone and then sighed. "OK. How long do you need? I could probably push the council for a while."

Shaking my head, I told him, "No, you can't. Or you shouldn't. Listen, my parents won't even be home, I'm sure. I can get in, take a shower, pack a bag, and get to work on time. Then after, I can come back here."

Whatever information the council had was crucial to knowing what was going on. Or at least that was what I thought. He needed to do that then go to work.

He folded his arms over his chest. "I'll go with you."

"Miller," I snapped, losing my patience. "You can't babysit me. You have a life."

"Protecting you *is* my life."

"If my parents haven't hurt me yet, why do you think they're going to now?" I waited, but before he could reply, I continued. "I know you all think they're being put under a lot of pressure to get me into the shadow coven or whatever, but how would hurting me help that? I'm not going to fall for any of their tricks. I'll text you when I get to work."

His jaw tightened. Clearly, he wasn't liking any of my ideas, but finally, he gave me a curt nod. "You need to spend as little time there as possible. There are things happening that you don't know about. People are getting desperate. Please be careful."

"Fine. I'll get clothes and come back here to shower."

"I'll leave the door unlocked and get you a key made today."

"OK." I pushed up from my seat and wrapped a hand around the amulet he'd given me. "Plus, I still have this. I won't take it off even for a second."

His firm hands closed over my hips as he pulled me toward him. He rested his head on my stomach. "If anything happens to you..."

"Nothing's going to happen to me." I gently pushed my hands into his hair. "Promise."

Though in any horror movie, those were famous last words. I wasn't worried. Miller had me as protected as he could and my parents weren't going to hurt me. That didn't mean I'd dick around at home. No way. I'd be in and out, but I needed underwear.

Miller pushed to his feet and threaded his fingers through my hair so he could bring my mouth to his.

If there was any doubt about how he felt about me, that kiss would've told me everything. He was gentle at first, but then he deepened it and his mouth became forceful. If I didn't know better, I would've thought he was trying to get me back into bed.

But there wasn't time for that.

"Text or call me when you get back here, OK?"

I nodded because I couldn't form words. That kiss had me reeling.

When I left Miller's apartment, he followed and for a minute, I thought he might trail me all the way to my house, which was exactly what I didn't want him to do

He didn't follow me. But he did stand there watching until I couldn't see him anymore.

It didn't take too long to get over to my house and as I had promised Miller, there was no one there.

Still, for some reason, I tried to be quiet. Like me making noise would trigger something and my parents would magically appear.

I was being an idiot.

It was only fifteen minutes later that I had my bag packed and was creeping back through the house to get the hell out of here. Now that Miller had told me his suspicions, the house made me uneasy and I felt like I was being watched. I'd heard the saying that the walls had ears, but never that they had eyes.

"Jesus Christ," I yelled, stepping back.

My mother was standing between me and the door where she, for sure, hadn't been when I'd come in. She had a hard look on her face that reminded me of Miss Hannigan from Annie. Id' never noticed the resemblance before.

"What're you doing?" I asked. "And why scare the shit out of me?"

"I'm not doing anything and you scared yourself," she said. Maybe she was right, but I wouldn't tell her that. "Where are you going?"

I lifted the bag further up my shoulder. "I'm staying at Miller's for a few nights." Nice, normal response. Lots of nineteen-year-olds stayed at their boyfriends' houses.

"You're not spending the night with him."

I raised an eyebrow. "I did last night."

Mom sighed then pinched the bridge of her nose the way she did when I was getting on her last nerve. "I thought I taught you to respect yourself more than that."

"I do. Miller respects the hell out of me, too."

"Hazel Riley! I don't want to hear that from you again."

I rolled my eyes. "Mother, I didn't mention the amount of time we spent in his bed naked. You took it there. I said he respects me. Now I have to go." I moved around her because I knew she wasn't going to try to stop me physically.

"Where?"

"I have to work today."

"In yesterday's clothes?"

Her words brought me to a stop. As far as I knew, I hadn't seen my parents yesterday. Which begged the question of how she knew that I'd been wearing this dress.

"I'm going to change at work."

"Hazel." She reached out to touch my arm. We weren't a touching kind of family, so it took me off guard. "I really need you to reconsider. Part of the fundraiser requires we bring our family. You listen to the charity and if you don't like what they say, you don't go back, but we have to bring you."

I raised an eyebrow at her. "That's a really weird thing for a charity to require. It's probably a pyramid scheme, Mom, and you should get out of it."

Her grip on me tightened. "I'm not playing around anymore, Hazel."

"Neither am I." I yanked my arm away so hard that she had to take a step back to keep from falling.

Then I left that house, hating that I'd ever have to return.

My parents were getting weirder by the day, which meant that everything Miller had told me was probably true.

I didn't think he'd been lying when he'd told me what his coven thought about my parents, but a little part of me hadn't believed him. My parents were weird, but not dark magic kind of people.

I was so wrong and blind to their lives that I had refused to see it.

Once back at Miller's, I sent him a text so he'd know that I was back safely, but I did leave out the interaction with my mother. If I told him, he'd rush home and probably keep me from going to work. With all of this happening, I still wanted us to have some normalcy.

Then I headed to the shower.

Thirty minutes later, I was dressed and ready to go to work. I'd pulled my hair into a bun so I wouldn't have to take the time to dry it.

But when I came out from the bedroom area and turned into the kitchen, someone grabbed me, slapped what felt suspiciously like duct tape over my mouth, then put a bag over my head.

I fought. I pulled and tried to scream, but the noise that came out was so muted by the tape, no one would hear me even if they had been home. Miller's amulet still hung around my neck as it was supposed to so this was even more confusing.

How could anyone have gotten me if I was under a protection spell?

"No one's home at the main house," the unfamiliar male voice whispered into my ear. "You can try to scream all you want."

Tears welled up in my eyes as I continued to fight, knowing that my energy was going to quickly deplete. Adrenaline would keep me going for now because the fear that had filled my heart was telling me that if I didn't fight, I might not live through it.

"Oh, keep fighting, little bird. We like it." That was a second voice that was distinctly creepier.

Little bird? What the fuck was that?

Between the two of them, they easily grabbed an arm and one leg each then lifted me off the ground.

Then we were outside. I could feel the sun on my legs and was suddenly thankful that I'd chosen to wear long shorts today. A skirt or dress would've been showing them way more than they had a right to see.

Or was that their intention anyway? Was this a BTK kind of thing? Who were these people? Were they in cahoots with my parents? The shadow coven?

A heavy sliding sound came from in front of us right after my feet had hit the ground. Then I was shoved inside of something. A van, by the feel of it. Then the door slid shut.

"What're you doing?" I asked, my voice quivering with the fear that I didn't want them to know I was experiencing. "Where are you taking me?"

"You'll find out soon enough."

Whoever was driving backed out of the driveway roughly then squealed the tires to take off toward town. Or I thought it was toward town. My brain was overprocessing everything. I was trying to take in every turn, every smell, every whispered word in the front. I swallowed hard when I thought of Miller. I was so overwhelmed that my mind completely blanked on any spell I could do to get myself out of this situation.

He'd been right to be worried about me, but it hadn't been going home that had turned out to be the problem. These men had taken me from his own apartment and I hated that for him.

I hated it worse for me, but he was going to blame himself.

I swallowed hard, trying to bring forward the bravery I knew I should have had. "Are you taking me to the shadow coven?"

A hand smacked me across my covered face. An explosion wracked my cheek up to my eye.

"Calm down," a third man said. "They don't want her hurt."

"Just keep your mouth shut." Asshole Number One must've been the one to hit me.

"Can I at least get this thing off my head?"

No one answered, but after some time had passed, and I failed at even trying to cast a single spell, the hood was pulled off.

The inside the van was dim, with the only light coming from the front windows. This was the kind of van that parents warned you not to park near at the grocery store.

Now I knew they had a reason to be worried.

"We're not going to hurt you," a fourth man assured me, but to say it didn't put me at ease was an understatement.

"You already have." I pushed myself up to a better position.

"Get her ready," the one driving called out and I didn't know what the hell that meant, but I didn't like the sound of it.

As the fourth man crawled toward me on his knees, I tried to push as far away from him as I could. When he reached out, I was prepared to bite him, gouge out his eyes, do something. But he didn't touch me the way I'd thought he was going to. He grabbed my amulet, yanked it off, then tossed it to the man in the passenger seat. That man rolled down his window and chucked it into oblivion.

"It was dead," he said as he rolled his window back up.

Miller had said he needed to recharge it but we'd gotten distracted.

Fuck.

Asshole Number Four said, "This is going to hurt."

Asshole Number Three grabbed my arm and held firm while the man I'd heard one of them call Seth pulled out the biggest horse needle I'd ever seen. He wiped my arm then jabbed the needle into it.

Burning-hot pain radiated up to my shoulder,

but I wouldn't give them the satisfaction of allowing the tears to fall.

"That will keep any of your coven friends from finding you and will make sure we can find you wherever you are, regardless of any cloaking spell.

"It's a tracker?" My voice cracked as he pulled the needle from my arm.

"Yup," Number Three told me. "So it's no use running."

The van came to an abrupt stop. Minutes later, I was pulled from the back with blood running down my arm into my hand. That needle had been huge and they hadn't even given me a Band-Aid. There was a door that looked like it would lead into a barn, but instead, right inside were stairs that they hauled me down.

It was everything I could do to keep from falling.

After a walk through interconnected hallways, we climbed a different set of stairs and I was thrust out into the sunlight.

There were so many people milling about. As I looked around, I found that there was a wall surrounding this place. It reminded me of the kind old castles had to keep out intruders. Women and men my age and a little younger hurried about as if they were late for classes.

It was a weird combination of Renaissance Festival vibes and high school.

One of the assholes pushed me to get me going. My feet didn't want to cooperate, but I made them as this group for idiots led me to a building across the courtyard.

Was this a sleepaway camp? That was what it reminded me of, but I'd seen an old movie called that once and no, thank you.

"Sit." Asshole Number Four pushed me into a chair then the four of them stood around me.

An older man with blond hair and these crazy, blue eyes came in and took a seat behind the desk.

"It's nice to finally meet you, Hazel," he said, as if I were there of my own free will. "We have a lot to talk about."

18

———

MILLER

Everything in me screamed to not leave Hazel alone.

But she wanted to have some normalcy. I thought she didn't want it to seem like I was her babysitter.

Still, I wished I would've gone to her house with her. Maybe I would've felt better if instead of enjoying her naked body last night, I would've recharged her amulet.

"What's got your panties knotted up?" Oliver asked when I entered the garage.

"Wishing I would've recharged Hazel's amulet last night."

Luken leaned on the hood of the car he was going to be working on today. "It's only been what? A couple of weeks? It's probably fine."

My muscles tightened. I hated the word *probably*. "I hope so."

"Besides..." Oliver nudged me five times with his elbow as he asked, "What were you doing last night that you couldn't recharge it?"

I pushed him hard enough that he took two steps. "Fuck off."

"We know what they were doing," Luken countered. "That's not the point. What's Hazel doing today?"

I told him the plan and he nodded as I spoke. "OK, then. I've got the bookstore covered. Nobody's going to your house, especially while your parents are home." Dad walked the through garage, giving the three of us a nod. "Or while your mom is home and she's got the amulet. Even if it's weakened, there's still coverage. She'll be fine."

"Yeah." Oliver shoved me back. "Now get your ass to work."

The three of us chuckled as we went to get our days started.

I had a new Ford to work on that just needed general maintenance, oil change, and new breaks. Luken had an old mustang that I' would've given my left nut to own and Oliver was rebuilding a motorcycle engine for a guy who was rebuilding a custom Harley.

We all had shit to do.

About an hour later, an ache formed in my chest like the time I'd dropped a weight bar on it. The guys and I had been in high school and had been fucking around with far too much weight. My mother had freaked out and told me that I could've killed myself.

This was worse.

I tried to brush it off and keep working, but within minutes, it was like this Ford was sitting on my chest.

After getting out from beneath it, I stood near my tool box rubbing my chest.

"What's wrong?" Luken asked, which brought Oliver over to me. "You hurt yourself?"

I shook my head and said, "But it feels like the fucking car is sitting on my chest and it's like I'm scared. But I'm not fucking scared of a Ford."

"Oh, shit. Hazel," Oliver muttered, his eyes wide and wild as he glanced out of the bay doors and then back.

I grabbed his shirt and hauled him close. "What the fuck did you do?"

"The night we made Hazel's amulet, I knew you two were going to be focused on the protection, so I went with an alert. I tied the amulet to you so that if she ever felt scared, you'd know."

"That's what this is?" I practically yelled.

"Has to be, but she's at work by now, right?"

I glanced at my phone, but I didn't know. She sure as hell wouldn't still be at her parents' house. "I have to get to the bookstore."

Then I took off in a run. The store was only a few blocks down from the garage and honestly, it would've taken longer for me to get in my car and go around than to just run there. So I did, leaving the guys in my dust.

I ran faster than I ever had before but was barely winded when I tore through the door on the front of the bookstore.

It was her boss at the register talking to an older woman whom I'd seen around town.

"Where's Hazel?" I asked, interrupting their conversation. Her boss furrowed her brows.

"I don't know," she told me. "She didn't show up for her shift and didn't call. It's really unlike her."

Before she finished talking, I had already turned and pulled my phone out of my pocket, hitting Hazel's contact.

It rang as Luken and Oliver caught up to me. But no one answered. I tried again, this time leaving a message telling her to call me as soon as she got this. That was when I remembered that she'd sent a text saying she was back at my apartment.

But she wasn't answering the phone.

"Where's the last place you knew she was?" Luken asked, keeping a much calmer head than I was.

"My place. She went to her parents to get her stuff then sent a text that she was going to take a shower."

"Then we have to go there," Oliver said.

The three of us jogged back to the garage, but before I could get in my car, my dad came out. "What's going on?" he asked.

"Hazel," I told him, but I let Oliver fill him in on the amulet and what I was feeling.

"Go," he said, waving us off. "I'll be right behind you."

Not wanting to argue with him and honestly, not wanting to discourage him from closing the garage for a while, I hopped into my car and brought it to life. Oliver did the same with his and Luken revved his motorcycle.

The three of us were off, like we were in the middle of a police chase.

I hit the curb when pulling into my driveway,

and the guys were right behind me. In a flash, the three of us were running up the stairs.

"Hazel," I called out after I'd come through the door. No answer. "Fuck."

I hurried to the bathroom, where it looked like she'd taken a shower earlier, but there were no signs of her now.

She wasn't in this apartment, but I found her phone in the kitchen and that was when I realized that the crushing feeling in my chest had disappeared.

"FUCK!" I yelled as I slammed my fist down on the countertop. "Her phone is here and the crushing is gone from my chest." I stomped over to Oliver. "What does that mean?"

"I don't know," he said quickly.

"It's your fucking spell."

"That doesn't mean I know what has to happen to stop the feeling."

"OK." Luken stepped between us and pushed us apart. "There's no point in arguing. If something's happened, Oliver's spell is the only reason you know it has. Now, what do we know?"

I ground my teeth together as my father joined us in the apartment.

"She's not at work," I said through clenched teeth. "She's not here, but her phone is."

"Her car's downstairs," Dad added and fuck me, I hadn't even thought to notice.

"Oliver linked her amulet to me, which is how I could feel that she's scared. Now it's gone." I looked at my dad. "What does that mean?"

He placed a hand on my shoulder and squeezed. "It means one of a couple of things. That the amulet lost power. That only happens if it hasn't been recharged or if someone draws the power out. Or she's taken it off."

"She promised she wouldn't."

"Someone could've done it for her," Luken offered, which was true but didn't help the whole rage thing I had going on. "You did say you needed to recharge it. That would mean someone could do it."

"Is that it?" I asked my dad.

He hesitated and looked at the guys before coming back to me. "No."

"What? Tell me."

"It wouldn't be able to transmit her feelings if she didn't have any."

Well, fuck. That didn't make sense. "Why the fuck wouldn't she have feelings?"

The three of them got quiet. Too fucking quiet.

I shook my head. "No. No fucking way is she dead. Her parents wouldn't do that because they want her for the shadow coven."

I wouldn't accept that until I saw the fucking body.

My stomach roiled with fear, anger, rage... everything I could be feeling at that moment.

"What do we do?" I asked Dad.

"You've looked everywhere?" he confirmed. I nodded. The only other place would be our spot in the woods, but she wouldn't go there. Not now. She'd been adamant about getting to work. "I'll have your mom scry for her. I already called her when I left the garage. She should be here any moment."

"I can't just sit here," I told him.

"No. I know. I've been where you are," he said. I furrowed my brows because I had no fucking idea what that meant, but now wasn't the time to figure it out. "We've got to see what the council knows. I can do that. You're still connected to the amulet, so you'll need to get grounded and lead yourself to it. Maybe she's with it."

"What if she's not?"

Dad took a minute to think over his answer. "We're all pretty sure the shadow coven is involved."

The three of us nodded. "Then we're going to find them and get her back." His eyes darkened. "Starting by confronting her parents."

The four of us headed outside. Dad was going to wait for Mom in the house. They'd call us if she learned anything.

I stood in the middle of the back yard, grounding myself to the earth. The breeze blew a little harder as I called on all the elements to tell me where the amulet was. Once I'd cleared my mind, which was hard to do when worry for my woman was consuming me, I felt the pull.

"Let's go," I told the guys.

Oliver hopped behind the wheel of my car and I got in the passenger side while Luken was back on his bike.

I wanted to drive myself, but I had to focus. Focus was what would lead me to Hazel or the amulet.

As I gave directions with my eyes closed, Oliver responded and a bit later, we were pulled over on the side of the road in an area with just farmland.

The three of us got out and I let the pull lead me.

There on the ground I found the onyx amulet that I'd given Hazel. It had been tossed aside, as if it didn't mean anything, or rather, tossed aside because it did.

Whoever had her knew exactly what that amulet did and they'd been sure to get rid of it so I wouldn't be able to find her.

And I wasn't there to protect her.

"FUCK!" I screamed into the air then silently promised Hazel that I wasn't going to give up.

One way or another, I was going to find her.

And I didn't care how many witches I had to kill to keep my promise.

19

HAZEL

"I DON'T KNOW YOU," I TOLD THE MAN IN FRONT OF me. "So I'm pretty sure we have nothing to talk about."

"Oh, but we do."

"Maybe I'd give you the time of day if your goons hadn't just kidnapped me and tossed me into a van like they were serial killers."

The sass came so naturally to me that I was pretty sure it was my defense mechanism. This man could've probably killed me with the flick of his finger, but that clearly wasn't his intention.

"To be fair," the man across from me continued, "we have tried to get you to come of your own free will for a while now, but you refused."

I narrowed my eyes on him. "So this is the

shadow coven?" I glanced around. "I'm not impressed."

The corners of his mouth turned up. "You will be. Though I'm not surprised that Miller told you everything."

My stomach clenched at the mention of Miller. He had to be so worried and scared for me. I wanted to kick myself for not just letting him go into work late.

"What do you want?" I pushed.

This creepy smile crossed his face. "You."

I winced, disgusted by the way that had sounded. "You're not my type."

He leaned forward, pressing his hands against one another. "Now, Hazel, you know that's not what I meant." He reached over his desk for a tissue then tossed it at me before resuming his position. "For the blood."

That was right. I was still bleeding. I took the tissue, folded it as thickly as I could, then pressed it against the puncture wound. The bleeding had mostly stopped by now anyway.

"You have something special inside you, Hazel. Something our coven could benefit from. Your parents have already pledged their allegiance to dark magic and it's time you did too. However, since you've been more resistant, there's something we need to do first." His teeth had given a weird hardness to the "T" in *resistant* that made me uncomfortable.

"And what's that? Because I'm never going to pledge myself to dark magic."

"You will." He brushed his hand through the air, as if my declaration meant nothing. "But first, we need to show you what all of this is about and that's why you're here."

"At sleepaway camp?"

He nodded. "Yes. This used to be a camp for children, but we bought it and it's now our home base." He pushed up from his chair to lean across the desk. "Here you will learn why this is the place for you. You will learn that we are the ones fighting for a way of life that the light witches are trying to take from us."

"This sounds a little like a civil war that I don't want to be part of."

"You will." He sounded so convinced that turning me dark would be so easy that I was starting to believe him.

No. I'd made promises to Miller.

Miller. He'd told me he loved me last night and at the time, I couldn't find the words. Now I was wishing he was in front of me so I could touch him and tell him that I loved him too.

My mother had said she didn't want me hurt, but I already had been. If this didn't go their way, I was no longer sure they wouldn't do something worse.

And I'd never get the chance to tell Miller that I loved him.

"Are you listening?" he snapped.

"No."

"You'd better start. You're here for the duration. You'll go through the program." Which I was sure was indoctrination. "At the end, you'll see the truth and come to our side."

"I'm glad you think so."

The door opened and my parents stepped through. My face burned with anger.

I was their daughter. How could they do this to me?

"Listen to him, Hazel," Mom pleaded.

"Why would I do what you want?" I asked her. "I'm your daughter." My eyes burned, but there was zero chance I'd allow any of them to see me cry. "How can you do this to me? I just wanted a normal life."

"You're not normal," Dad told me.

Was he saying that I was the special unicorn sent

to save everyone? No. I didn't think so, but I also knew he wouldn't have answered if I asked what he'd meant.

"Miller was right all along," I said instead. "When he told me that he thought you were part of the shadow coven, I didn't believe him at first. But he was right and all I was to you was someone you could bring in." I shook my head. "Do you even love me?"

"Of course we do." Mom took a step closer but then stopped. "But we need you to join the coven so we can be a real family."

I swallowed hard and shook my head. "I don't want to be your family. Miller is my family."

"Miller Campbell is out of your life," the man snapped. "Let's move on."

He moved back to his desk and motioned for me to sit back down like he was. I did it because right now, I wasn't sure what else to do. Then I focused, trying to send Miller a mental message. He'd said that some witches could do that, though I'd never been one.

"Your magic isn't going to work here," the man behind the desk said. He hadn't given me a name and it'd gone on so long that I started to think it had been on purpose. "We have this place heavily warded. There are certain areas where it will work, but that will only be under close supervision." He sat back, looking like a villain out of a movie. "Let's get to the rules."

"Rules? Why would I follow your rules?"

"Because if you don't, you won't like the consequences." Well, that didn't sound fun. "Now, your magic won't work. You had a tracker implanted so that even if you were able to skirt our very powerful scrying, we'd still find you. You leave, and there's nowhere you can go where we won't get you back. You will learn. You will obey. And most of all, at the end, you will comply." He sat forward. "Now, also the tracker is programmed for where you are allowed on the compound. If a door doesn't unlock when you get there, you're not allowed in. We control that and we can also make it not open your cabin door for you."

"So this is prison."

"You may call it whatever you like, but this is to ensure you don't hurt yourself."

I snorted.

"You will be sharing a cabin with three other girls who will also be punished should you step out of line."

"That's fucked-up," I told him. Any of us being

responsible for the actions of any of the rest of us was fucked up. There was no way around that.

"Now," he said, as if he hadn't heard a word I'd spoken. "There are consequences for stepping out of line and I have a feeling that you're going to discover most of them."

I held back a smile. He thought I was going to be a troublemaker and he was right. I wasn't going to fall into the cult mindset that was going on around here.

"Hazel," Mom said, bringing my attention to her as she sat in the chair beside me and reached for my hand. I wouldn't let her take it, but she tried. "You have to cooperate. At least consider what we have to offer. If you don't... at the end... we'll have to cut all contact. We can't force you into the coven."

Well, that all sounded great to me.

"You could get hurt if you don't join us," Mom said.

"I don't care," I told her honestly. "I'd rather be dead in a ditch than part of whatever you have going on here."

"That can be arranged," one of the assholes whom I'd forgotten were still in the room muttered.

Mom gave him a hard look then focused back in on me. "You're not the only one. Miller and his family will become targets and the coven will not stop until we have their blood in revenge for poisoning your mind. We need you to cooperate as you go through the program."

I felt like I was going to vomit. Acid filled my throat and my mouth began to water.

If I was the only one at risk, I was fine with that.

Miller and his family... that was a different story.

"OK," I agreed, already knowing that I was still going to try to find a way out of this, but I couldn't risk Miller or his parents. "I'll cooperate."

Mom's face lit up as I hadn't seen it do in a very long time. She leaned over and kissed the side of my head. "That's a good girl."

Her words disgusted me. Her touch angered me.

I'd told them that I'd cooperate with the program, but I was going to do everything I could to find my way out, ruin it for them, whatever came to mind.

If in the end I was unsuccessful, at least I wouldn't go down without a fight. If I failed, then I failed.

And if I had to join the dark coven to protect Miller and his parents, it would be worth it.

BONUS SCENE

I hope you enjoyed Cursed Magic as much as I enjoyed writing it. There was something I needed to work out first.

Who exactly are the shadow coven and what do they want? What other darkness have they been up to?

So, I wrote a novella that I'm offering to you! Now, it won't answer all the questions because if it did, why would we need more books. But, it will show you exactly how dark they can be.

All you have to do is sign up for my newsletter and you'll get an email giving you this novella!

https://dl.bookfunnel.com/9l4n92llak

He was my brother's best friend and off limits.

The world knows Silas Briggs as the baseball heartthrob on a hot streak. I know him as brother's former friend and my teenage crush.
Four years ago, he broke my young heart by making me think there could be something between us.

Then he left town and never looked back.

Now I'm back and working for the team, hoping that we can be friendly. Then I see him in person and friendship is the last thing on my mind.

START READING KISSING THE PLAYER TODAY

Do you love rock stars?

FOREVER GRAYSON

Forever 18 Book 1

One night three years ago is coming back to haunt me.

It was supposed to be one night then I'd never see him again. One night at a dive bar where I met someone who could scratch an itch.

He wasn't famous then.

Now he's a rock star.

A rock star whose manager just hired me to be the band's stylist. It's a dream job to me but it could be a nightmare.
Is it worse if he remembers me? Or worse if he doesn't?

START READING FOREVER GRAYSON NOW

Love your rock stars? Check out...
Daisy *Pushing Daisies Book 1*

Is it weird that I'm in a band with my brothers?
Not to me.

When I'm moved off our bus and onto the one that belongs to the hot manager of the headlining band, I know something's wrong.

Lawson is willing to take me on so some crazy fan can't get to me but when things heat up... he backs off. Says he's too old for me.

It's a small age gap. It doesn't mean a thing.

START READING DAISY NOW

Cross *Courting Chaos Book 1*

When a sexy drummer mistakes me for a groupie and tries to kick me out of the venue, I'm willing to chalk it up to mistaken identity. Usually everyone knows me but I shouldn't assume. Now Cross wants to make it right ini the hope that my father won't kick his band off the tour.

In trying to make amends, Cross becomes my surprise protector when I accidentally snap some pictures of his bandmate in a bad situation and he wants them deleted.

Cross being my protector has me wanting something I've never wanted before... A sexy drummer.

Growing up with a famous father has taught me many things but the number one rule has always been NEVER FALL FOR A ROCK STAR.

I guess I want to break the rules.

START READING CROSS TODAY

After living under my father's rule, I'm about to break free.

My father has kept me on a short leash my entire life.

The Orin comes for me.

Finding out what he is... scares the hell out of me.

Finding out I'm his supposed mate... I don't know that I'll recover.

START READING MOONSTRUCK TODAY

Being the daughter of my people's leaders, I should understand protocol and appropriate behavior. Problem is, I understand both, I just don't follow them.

But I have a different plan.

There's a boy... now a man, who is supposed to be powerful. I want him on our side.

What I didn't know is that together, he and I might be unstoppable.

Now I just have to find him.

START READING THE GREMLIN PRINCE TODAY

I'm a witch. Or so they tell me.

Finding out I'm a witch isn't even the weirdest part of my day. Having the guy who hated me in high school stand before me to tell me that I am, is.

Somehow, I'm supposed to learn spells and how to ground myself to the elements, fight the fact that I want him like I want air, and not freak out that my parents are part of a shadow coven trying to pull me over to the dark side.

Yeah. No problem.

START READING CURSED MAGIC TODAY

THE HARBOR POINT SERIES

A new adult contemporary romance series

Meet Gio and Sal.

Two damaged men who meet the woman who can set them right.

Then there's Cash.

He's not damaged but he's ready to do the healing when he meets Gemma.

START READING LOVE BY THE SLICE TODAY

THE FALLOUT SERIES

A new adult romance series

Coming home is hard.

Finding out the boy you loved had a baby with your

former best friend... heartbreaking.

START READING LAST GOOD THING TODAY

GAMBLING ON LOVE

A new adult romance series

Desperate times call for desperate measures so Flannery Tate is selling her virginity.

START READING HIGHEST BIDDER TODAY

I you'd like to just keep up with my sales and new releases, you can follow me on BookBub!

Bookbub: https://www.bookbub.com/authors/ heather-young-nichols

Heather Young-Nichols is a USA Today Bestselling author of contemporary and paranormal romances. She writes swoony heroes and snarky heroines with a heap of romance.

When she's not writing, she's binging a show with her kids, watching baseball, or snuggling with her cuddly animals.

Find Heather on Social Media or by visiting her website.

heatheryoungnichols.com

facebook.com/heatheryoungnicholsauthor

instagram.com/heatheryoungnichols

amazon.com/Heather-Young-Nichols/e/B00KKTM54A

bookbub.com/authors/heather-young-nichols

tiktok.com/@heatheryoungnichols

www.ingramcontent.com/pod-product-compliance
Lightning Source LLC
Chambersburg PA
CBHW021139310726

48971CB00002B/395